JOURNEY TO NOTHING

FROM GROUNDED TO GALACTIC

SAKSHAM MEHRA

Made with ♥ on the Notion Press Platform
www.notionpress.com

To the dreamers, the stargazers, and the curious minds who dare to question.

Contents

PROLOGUE

From an early age, I found myself captivated by the vastness of space, a fascination ignited by the adventures of Doraemon on other planets. This beloved cartoon not only entertained me but also opened my mind to the infinite possibilities that lie beyond our planet. It made me realize that the universe is not just a collection of stars and planets; it is a boundless realm of questions waiting to be explored. As I grew older, however, I encountered the rigid structures of the educational system. I often felt constrained by a curriculum that prioritized memorization over exploration. In a world where we are taught to adhere to prescribed knowledge, I struggled to understand why we weren't encouraged to ask bigger questions or pursue our passions. The system made me feel obligated to learn material that, while often important, did not resonate with my desire to explore the mysteries of the cosmos.

This book is my response to that disconnect. It is a manifestation of my journey to seek knowledge beyond the confines of traditional education. I believe that learning should be an adventure-one that ignites curiosity and inspires discovery. Through this work, I aim to share my passion for space and the importance of looking beyond the stars. I want readers to understand that the universe is filled with wonders waiting to be uncovered. My hope is that this book will encourage you to embrace your curiosity, question what you've been taught, and embark on your own journey of exploration. In a time when knowledge is more accessible than ever, let us not forget that true learning is driven by passion, wonder, and the courage to ask questions. Together, let us explore the mysteries of the universe and seek our own truths among the stars.

ACKNOWLEDGEMENTS

I want to thank my parents. From the very beginning, you encouraged my love for science and storytelling. Whether it was buying me space books, staying up late to watch space documentaries with me, or answering my endless questions about how the universe works, you nurtured my passion. Without your guidance and belief in my dreams, I would never have had the courage to embark on this journey.

Finally, to my readers: thank you for choosing to join me on this adventure. My dream is to share the knowledge and awe I feel for the universe with as many people as possible, and I hope this book sparks in you the same excitement I've felt ever since watching those first Doraemon episodes. May we all continue to look up, wonder, and never stop asking questions.

I

“Arwin, look at this page of the book!” Kelvin exclaimed, his voice a mix of excitement and disbelief.

“It says that if you want to make a time machine, you have to play with light or with the mind.”

Arwin’s brow furrowed in confusion. “Oh, but how is that possible?”

Kelvin leaned closer, his eyes wide. “There’s an example in this book! It explains that the stars we see in the sky—many of them are already dead. They’re thousands of light-years away, so it takes that long for their light to reach us. This means we’re looking at thousands of years in the past!”

Arwin’s mouth fell open, the enormity of the concept hitting him like a wave. He exchanged a stunned glance with Kelvin, both feeling the weight of this revelation.

“So, we’re literally time travelers, just by looking up at the stars?”

“Exactly!” Kelvin replied, his voice barely above a whisper. The realization hung between them, a mixture of awe and disbelief. They continued to stare at each other, the shock of the idea settling in as they pondered the implications of what it meant to witness the past in real time.

"Here's something else!" Kelvin said, flipping the page with urgency. "It says that at the beginning of the universe, there was nothing—everything was compressed into a single dot. Then, there was an explosion called the Big Bang, and with that, everything we know came into existence. Before that, there wasn't even time!"

Arwin furrowed his brow, trying to grasp the enormity of it all. "But how can everything be contained in just a dot?" His mind raced with questions, the sheer scope of the idea feeling both thrilling and overwhelming.

Kelvin nodded, excitement flickering in his eyes. "Exactly! We need to find answers to these questions. But every time we go to Mr. Caldwell, our physics teacher, he just brushes us off. He says it's outside our syllabus and that we don't need to study it. It's such a waste of time, he thinks."

Arwin felt a surge of frustration. "It's not a waste of time! This is the stuff that could change everything we know about reality. How can he not see that?"

"I know!" Kelvin replied, exasperated. "It feels like he's stifling our curiosity. We're trying to explore something bigger than ourselves, and all he cares about is what's in the textbook."

Arwin sighed, leaning back against the desk. "Maybe we should find someone else to talk to. There have to be other resources or people who would understand. This is too important to just let go."

Kelvin considered this, a spark of determination lighting up his face. "You're right! We can't let this be the end of our exploration. There has to be someone who would be willing to help us."

With their minds racing and hearts set on discovery, they began brainstorming ways to pursue the answers that had eluded them in the classroom. The thrill of the unknown beckoned them, and together, they were determined to uncover the truths that lay hidden in the universe.

"Arwin, it's 1 PM! We have English class," Kelvin said, glancing at his watch with urgency. "We're going to be late, and you know Mrs. Paul will scold us."

"Okay, but please wait a minute. I have to issue this book," Arwin replied, his eyes fixed on the fascinating volume they had been exploring. "I want to read it all, and we can talk about it tonight."

Kelvin sighed but nodded, understanding how important this was to Arwin. They quickly made their way to the library counter. "Excuse me, ma'am, we'd like to issue this book," Arwin said, placing it on the counter.

The librarian looked up, adjusting her glasses. "Sure, but you need to return it by next week. If it's not returned on time, there will be a fine."

Arwin nodded earnestly. "We'll make sure to return it on time, I promise."

"Alright, just sign here," she instructed, sliding a clipboard toward him.

As Arwin scribbled his name, he felt a surge of anticipation. "Thanks so much!" he said, turning to Kelvin. "Let's hurry to class now."

With the book safely in hand, they rushed out of the library, their minds still buzzing with the possibilities waiting to be explored.

As they entered the classroom, Arwin and Kelvin exchanged eager glances, the excitement of their earlier discoveries still fresh in their minds. The bell rang, signaling the start of the period, and just then, Mrs. Paul walked in, her presence commanding immediate attention.

"Alright, everyone, settle down!" she said, her voice firm yet inviting. "You two, sit down," she directed toward Arwin and Kelvin, who quickly made their way to the last bench. They chose the back row strategically, hoping it would give them a little cover to dive into the book without being easily noticed.

Once seated, Arwin pulled the book, flipping it open to the pages they had been exploring earlier.

"There's something incredible in this book!" Arwin whispered excitedly, his eyes gleaming as he pointed to a passage. "It says that space agencies are planning to send humans to Mars!"

Kelvin leaned in closer, his interest piqued. "Really? That's amazing! We could be the first humans to set foot on Mars!"

"Can you imagine?" Arwin continued, his voice barely above a whisper, brimming with enthusiasm. "Exploring a whole new planet, seeing the landscape, feeling the Martian soil beneath our feet.

Kelvin nodded, his imagination igniting at the thought. "Yes, for sure! Mars is just waiting for us to reach it. Think of all the discoveries we could make there! It would be historic."

As they exchanged their thoughts, they could hardly contain their excitement. The idea of being part of such a monumental event felt exhilarating, like they were on the brink of a new frontier.

"What do you think it would be like?" Arwin mused, picturing the red, dusty terrain and the vast Martian sky. "Would it be all barren, or could there be something hidden beneath the surface?"

"Maybe there's life!" Kelvin suggested, his eyes wide. "Even if it's just microscopic, it would change everything we know about the universe. It could prove that we're not alone."

"Exactly! And the technology we'd need to get there—imagine being part of a team that creates that!" Arwin's voice was filled with awe.

As they spoke, the classroom faded away,

"But there will be very few chances of coming back," Kelvin said, a hint of seriousness creeping into his voice.

Arwin paused, considering the implications. "If it came down to it, and the only option was to go to Mars and never come back, I'd still do it," he said, a fierce determination shining in his eyes. "It would be an adventure of a lifetime! I want to explore the unknown, no matter the cost."

Kelvin nodded slowly, feeling the weight of Arwin's words. "You know what? Me too. If it's a chance to make history, I'd take it. There's so much out there waiting to be discovered."

"Okay, then," Arwin declared, his excitement returning. "We'll go together! No matter what, we'll face it as a team."

A grin spread across Kelvin's face, the thrill of their shared resolve igniting their imaginations. "We'll be the first humans on Mars! Just think about it—our names in the history books, exploring a whole new world. We'll figure everything out together."

They exchanged high-fives, their hearts racing at the thought of their bold decision. The classroom around them faded further into the background, replaced by visions of red landscapes, Martian sunsets, and the thrill of the unknown.

The weight of their English lesson lost in the thrill of possibilities. With every word, they felt more connected to the universe and the future they could help shape. The idea of venturing to Mars wasn't just a dream; it felt like a tangible goal, a journey waiting for them just beyond the horizon.

Tenses in English—past, present, and future," she announced, writing key terms on the board. Her handwriting was neat and precise, each letter crisp against the whiteboard. "Understanding tenses is crucial for conveying the right meaning in our writing. Who can tell me the difference between the simple past and the present perfect tense?"

"Kelvin and Arwin, what are you doing back there?" Mrs. Paul's voice cut through their excitement like a sharp bell. She pointed at them, an eyebrow raised, a mix of curiosity and authority in her expression.

They froze for a moment, exchanging wide-eyed looks before bursting into nervous laughter. "Uh, nothing!" Kelvin replied quickly, trying to suppress the grin that threatened to break out.

Mrs. Paul approached their bench, crossing her arms. "Really? It looked like you were plotting something. High-fives, huh?"

The class erupted into laughter, the sound echoing off the walls.

Arwin leaned forward, trying to regain his composure. "We were just... discussing our plans for a science project!" he stammered, his heart racing.

"Science project, you say?" Mrs. Paul's expression softened slightly, though she still looked skeptical. "Well, as long as you're engaged in something productive. Just remember, this is an English class."

"Yes, ma'am!" they chorused, trying to sound earnest while their minds were still buzzing with visions of Mars.

With a final scrutinizing glance, Mrs. Paul returned to the front of the class. "Alright, let's get back to tenses, shall we?"

Arwin quickly tucked the science book into his bag, his fingers brushing over the cover as if to hold onto the excitement a moment longer. He took a deep breath, reminding himself to focus on Mrs. Paul as she continued her lesson about tenses.

"Alright, class," she said, her tone firm yet inviting, "let's review the different tenses we discussed. Who can tell me the example from the present perfect?"

A girl in the front row, her hand shooting up eagerly, stood up with confidence. "I have one!" she called out, her voice clear and assertive. "I have visited the museum many times."

Mrs. Paul nodded, her eyes sparkling with approval. "Great example! That's the present perfect tense in action. It shows an action that started in the past and continues to have relevance now."

The class murmured in appreciation, and Arwin couldn't help but admire her enthusiasm. He felt a slight pang of regret for not being more engaged in the lesson, especially as the girl returned to her seat, a satisfied smile on her face.

"Can anyone provide an example of the simple past tense?" Mrs. Paul continued, glancing around the room.

Just as Mrs. Paul asked for another example, the bell rang, cutting through the classroom like a release of pent-up energy. The sound echoed off the walls, and a wave of relief washed over the students.

"Alright, everyone, that's it for today!" Mrs. Paul said, her tone shifting to a lighter note. "Don't forget to review your tenses for homework!"

The teacher gathered her things and left the classroom. A flurry of movement followed as students hurried to pack their bags, eager to escape into the afternoon. Books were shoved into backpacks, chairs scraped against the floor, and the excited chatter of plans for the evening filled the air.

Arwin moved more slowly, lost in thought as he zipped up his bag. Across the room, Kelvin waved at him, weaving through the sea of students as they made their way toward the corridor.

"Arwin! Wait up!" he called, catching up to his friend.

"Hey, come over to my house today," Kelvin suggested with a bright grin. "We can talk about the universe, maybe even come up with our own theories about black holes or parallel dimensions. I've got this new space documentary you have to see!"

Arwin smiled faintly at the offer but hesitated. "I'd love to, but... I've got a cricket match tomorrow," he said, his voice lacking the usual excitement. "And today's practice too, so I won't be able to come." The words felt hollow as they left his mouth, and even though he was talking about cricket—something he used to love—it didn't stir the same thrill anymore.

There was a time when Arwin couldn't wait to get on the field, feeling the rush of the game, the camaraderie of his teammates, the satisfaction of a well-placed shot. But now, the excitement that had once filled his chest before a match was gone. Instead, his thoughts were consumed by stars, planets, and distant galaxies. Cricket, which used to be his favorite escape, now seemed... dull.

As they walked down the corridor, Arwin realized something had shifted inside him. The idea of running around a grassy field, batting and bowling under the afternoon sun, paled in comparison to the vast mysteries of space. Thinking about the universe with Kelvin, dreaming of Mars, of worlds far beyond their own—that was where his heart was now.

As they reached the school gates, Kelvin turned to Arwin with a casual smile. "Alright then, I guess we'll catch up later. Maybe we can talk about that documentary tonight?"

Arwin nodded, trying to shake off the strange feeling that lingered in his chest. "Yeah, let's talk tonight," he agreed, though his mind was still swirling with thoughts of space and his waning excitement for cricket.

Kelvin gave him a light punch on the shoulder. "Don't let the match get you down. We'll figure out the mysteries of the universe after."

Arwin managed a small smile. "Yeah, for sure."

With that, they waved goodbye and went their separate ways, each disappearing into the crowd of students heading home.

After parting ways with Kelvin, Arwin made his way home, his mind still adrift in thoughts of space. The familiar streets felt distant today, like he was walking through them on autopilot, barely noticing the usual sounds of kids playing or the hum of passing cars. He reached his front door and rang the bell, the chime snapping him back to the present.

Welcome home, my boy!" she said, her voice filled with the kind of warmth only a mother can give. Her eyes lit up when she saw him, and she reached out, gently brushing a stray lock of his hair back into place as she often did when he came home. "How was school today?"

Arwin managed a small smile, though his mind was still a little foggy. "It was alright," he said, his voice soft.

His mother didn't press for more, sensing he needed a moment. Instead, she offered him a comforting pat on the shoulder. "Well, come in. Go wash your hands; lunch is ready. I made your favorite!" she added, hoping to lift his spirits with the promise of a good meal.

The familiar scent of food drifted from the kitchen, filling the hallway with warmth. Normally, it would have sparked joy in him, but today Arwin just nodded. "Thanks, Mom," he replied quietly.

"Go on, wash up," she urged gently, her smile never fading. "You've had a long day. Lunch will help."

Her soft, caring tone made him feel a little better as he made his way to the bathroom. Even though his thoughts were still tangled up in space and the upcoming cricket match, the way his mother greeted him—so full of love and familiarity—grounded him, if only for a moment.

After washing his hands, Arwin headed to the dining area, where his mother had already set the table. The aroma of his favorite dish filled the room, but today, it did little to lift his mood. He sat down and, without much thought, began eating, his mind still swirling with distant thoughts.

His mother glanced at him as she tidied up the kitchen, noticing how quickly he was eating. "You're in a rush today," she said lightly, though it seemed more like a comment than a question.

Arwin just nodded, barely tasting his food as he finished the last bite.

"Yeah, I just want to finish reading that book," he muttered, already thinking about the thick volume he'd borrowed from the school library.

As soon as Arwin finished his last bite, he quickly pushed his plate aside. He ran toward his school bag, which was still lying near the door where he'd dropped it earlier, and eagerly unzipped it. His fingers quickly found the book nestled between his notebooks and pens, and he pulled it out with a sense of anticipation. The cover showed a swirling galaxy, brilliant and colorful, inviting him into the depths of space and rushed toward his room, barely acknowledging his mother's presence in the kitchen.

He opened it eagerly without bothering to change out of his school uniform, the crisp pages inviting him in like a portal to another world. As he settled back against his pillows, he began to read, his eyes darting across the lines filled with descriptions of celestial bodies, theories about life beyond Earth, and the mind-bending possibilities of space travel.

Just as he was getting absorbed in the chapter, his mother's voice interrupted his thoughts. "Arwin," she called from the kitchen, "pack your cricket bag! It's 4 p.m., and your practice will start soon."

Arwin blinked, momentarily pulled back to reality. He glanced at the clock on the wall and saw it ticking closer to practice time. A part of him wanted to ignore it, to keep reading, to lose himself in the universe. But another part knew he had to go.

"Okay, Mom," he replied, closing the book reluctantly. The excitement he had once felt for cricket seemed to have evaporated, replaced by a desire to stay in the world of space exploration. Still, he knew he couldn't avoid the practice.

With a sigh, he got up and made his way to the closet, pulling out his cricket bag. As he packed it, his thoughts drifted back to the book, to the stars, to the distant worlds he longed to learn more about.

With a reluctant sigh, Arwin placed the book gently into the drawer of his bedside table, its colorful cover peeking out like a hidden treasure waiting for his return. The thought of the vast universe he had just explored lingered in his mind as he closed the drawer with a soft click, a promise to return to that adventure later.

He quickly changed out of his school uniform, peeling off the stiff button-up shirt and trousers that felt like a weight on his shoulders. In their place, he donned his white cricket dress, the fabric light and airy against his skin. .

Stepping into the hallway, Arwin found his mother in the kitchen, her back turned as she tidied up. "Mom, I'm heading out!" he called, his voice echoing slightly in the quiet house.

"Okay, sweetheart! Have fun!" she replied, turning to face him with a warm smile. "But remember, be careful out there."

II

As Arwin made his way to the cricket ground, his mind drifted far from the game he was about to play. Instead, he found himself lost in thoughts of Mars, the red planet shimmering in his imagination like a distant dream. He pictured himself aboard a sleek spacecraft, hurtling through the cosmos, the vast expanse of space stretching infinitely around him.

What would it be like to set foot on that rusty terrain, to be one of the first humans to explore its mysteries? He envisioned the crowd back home, family and friends beaming with pride as they gathered to hear about his journey. He could almost hear their voices asking for autographs, clamoring to touch a piece of his history.

"Arwin, the first human on Mars!" he imagined them saying, his name echoing through time as a symbol of exploration and bravery.

But just as he was savoring this daydream, the reality of his surroundings began to take shape. He turned a corner and arrived at the cricket ground, the familiar sounds of the game pulling him back to Earth. Players were scattered across the field: some were running laps, while others practiced their catches, the thwack of leather on palm ringing out in the air.

Suddenly, the coach's voice boomed across the field, breaking through his reverie. "Arwin! Come fast! Our practice has started!"

The urgency in the coach's tone snapped him back to reality. With a reluctant sigh, Arwin jogged toward the group, shaking off the remnants of his cosmic daydream. He joined his teammates, who were buzzing with energy, their laughter and chatter a stark contrast to the thoughts of interplanetary adventures that still lingered in his mind. He tried to focus on the practice, but the allure of Mars still tugged at him, a constant reminder of the dreams that stretched beyond the confines of the cricket field.

Arwin joined the practice reluctantly, still trying to shake off the lingering thoughts of Mars. He jogged into position as the coach directed the players, his body moving automatically while his mind wandered light-years away.

"Let's go, Arwin! High catches!" the coach barked, tossing the ball high into the air.

Arwin fixed his gaze on the soaring ball, but as it ascended, his thoughts took a familiar detour. He imagined himself standing on the dusty surface of Mars, the pale sun casting an eerie glow over the alien landscape. There, in the thinner atmosphere and with the planet's weaker gravity, everything would feel different. The ball, if tossed high into the Martian sky, would take longer to come down, drifting lazily toward the surface. He pictured it floating almost weightlessly, like something out of a dream.

He smiled to himself, imagining how easy it would be to catch a ball on Mars. No rush, no hurried reflexes—just patience as the ball gracefully descended. Here on Earth, it came down fast, but on Mars... he'd have all the time in the world. He'd be the best cricketer on Mars, the champion of slow-motion catches, his team cheering as he made every play look effortless.

But just as his thoughts reached that distant planet, the ball thudded into his palm, jolting him back to reality. It was heavier than he expected—an earthbound reminder that he wasn't on Mars yet.

"Focus, Arwin!" the coach yelled, noticing his distant expression.

Arwin nodded, blinking as he tried to refocus on the practice. But even as he continued, fielding ball after ball, the thought of how it would all feel different on Mars—how everything could change in the blink of an eye—stayed with him. The pull of gravity, the pull of reality, they both felt heavy today.

"Will you play like this tomorrow?" the coach shouted, hands on his hips, glaring across the field. His voice carried over the sounds of his teammates practicing nearby, causing them to pause and glance toward him.

Arwin blinked, the distant dreams of space and Mars crashing back to Earth with the weight of his missed catch. His heart sank, and he could feel the warmth of embarrassment creeping into his cheeks.

"I'm sorry, Coach," Arwin muttered, bending down to retrieve the ball. His mind felt heavy, clouded by the pull between his love for the game and the overpowering lure of his dreams of the stars.

After three grueling hours of practice, Arwin felt every muscle in his body ache with exhaustion. The sun had dipped lower in the sky, casting long shadows over the field as the team began to disperse. Sweat clung to his skin, his cricket whites stained with grass and dirt from diving and running drills, but the real weight he carried wasn't physical—it was the mental fatigue of fighting against his own thoughts all afternoon.

Each catch, each run, each shout from the coach had brought him back to the ground, back to reality. But even through the exhaustion, his heart wasn't in it. His mind kept drifting back to the wonders of space, to the dream of something far bigger than cricket matches and practices.

As he slung his kit over his shoulder and made his way off the field, Arwin's legs felt heavy, each step pulling him further from the idea that cricket held any real meaning for him anymore. The excitement he once felt for the game was fading, replaced by the powerful pull of his dreams about the stars. The bat and ball felt too small, too limiting compared to the vastness of the universe he longed to explore.

He let out a tired sigh, walking home in the fading light, his thoughts loud in the quiet streets.

I won't play cricket anymore, he told himself firmly. The decision surprised him at first, but as the words repeated in his mind, they settled in with a kind of clarity. What's the point?

He shook his head, his thoughts whirling. From now on, I'll focus on my studies—on space, science, the universe. His heart quickened at the thought. He imagined himself pouring over books about astronomy, physics, and the cosmos, the same books that ignited his passion just hours ago.

The thought of Mars flickered in his mind again. I don't need cricket when there are bigger things out there—things that matter.

Arwin walked on, determined, though a small pang of uncertainty still clung to the back of his mind. But for now, as he headed home, he felt a sense of peace with his decision. The stars, the planets, the mysteries of the universe—those would be his new playing field.

But even as he steeled himself with this new resolve, he knew he couldn't just make such a decision alone. He would have to tell his parents. Not today though, he thought, feeling the weight of that conversation press against him. His parents always encouraged him to follow his passions, but quitting cricket, a sport they'd supported him in for so long, would be a surprise. He needed to make sure it was the right decision—and for that, he needed to talk to Kelvin first.

Here's an extended version incorporating Arwin's decision to speak with Kelvin first and then his parents:

As Arwin trudged along the path home, the fading light casting long shadows on the street, his thoughts crystallized with each step. He had made up his mind: cricket no longer held the same magic for him. It wasn't that he didn't enjoy the game, but compared to the vastness of the universe, it just seemed so small—insignificant, even.

I'll focus on my studies, he thought again, the idea growing stronger, more resolute. Space, Mars, the stars—those were what really mattered to him. His future wasn't on a cricket field; it was out there, in the cosmos, where his dreams lived.

But even as he steeled himself with this new resolve, he knew he couldn't just make such a decision alone. He would have to tell his parents. Not today though, he thought, feeling the weight of that conversation press against him. His parents always encouraged him to follow his passions, but quitting cricket, a sport they'd supported him in for so long, would be a surprise. He needed to make sure it was the right decision—and for that, he needed to talk to Kelvin first.

I'll talk to Kelvin tomorrow, Arwin decided, nodding to himself as if to cement the plan.

I'll play one last match, he thought. He couldn't just walk away without a proper goodbye. Tomorrow's game would be his final one, a way to honor the sport that had once meant so much to him, even if his heart now belonged to the stars.

"I'll play the last cricket match tomorrow," Arwin said quietly to himself, as if speaking it aloud made it more real. He would give it his best, one last time, and then he would be free to pursue the path that truly called to him.

After that, no more cricket practices, no more matches. It was time to focus on something bigger. After tomorrow, he thought, I'll focus on my studies. On Mars. On my dream.

When Arwin finally reached home, the warm glow of the house lights greeted him through the windows. He stepped inside, without much thought, he shrugged the cricket bag off his shoulder and dropped it unceremoniously by the door, letting it fall where it landed. The heavy thud of the kit hitting the floor barely registered in his mind. The familiar scent of dinner wafting through the air.

His father was the first to speak, glancing over at him with a familiar, warm smile. "Hey, Arwin! How was practice today?" he asked. There was a subtle excitement in his tone. "Are you all set for tomorrow's match? Big game, right?"

Arwin paused, his fingers tightening around the straps of his cricket bag. For a moment, he felt the weight of his father's expectations hanging in the air, and the pressure of what he was about to say seemed heavier than before. He wasn't ready to share his decision just yet. He still needed to talk to Kelvin, to sort out his thoughts completely before bringing it up.

He forced a small smile and nodded. "Yeah, practice was okay," he said, though the words felt hollow. "I'm ready for tomorrow." The answer came out automatically, but even as he said it, the excitement that used to accompany those words was absent.

His father smiled, unaware of the internal conflict his son was wrestling with. "That's great, Arwin! Play your best tomorrow. You've been practicing hard for this."

Arwin nodded again, but inside, he knew that tomorrow would be different. It wouldn't just be another match—it would be his last. He was already thinking about what he'd say to Kelvin tomorrow and how he'd explain everything to his parents once the match was over.

After nodding to his father, Arwin set down his cricket bag by the door and walked over to the dining table, where his parents were still seated. He glanced over at his mom, who was flipping through the pages of her magazine, her mind half on the television and half on dinner preparations.

"Mom," he said, his voice breaking through the quiet hum of the TV. "What's in the dinner?"

His mother looked up, smiling warmly at him. "I made your favorite," she said, gesturing toward the kitchen. "Spaghetti with garlic bread, and there's some salad too.

The heaviness of the day—practice, his thoughts of quitting cricket, the mental tug-of-war—faded for a moment. He felt a surge of happiness. Spaghetti was his favorite, and after hours on the field, the thought of it made his stomach rumble.

His face brightened, and he leaned forward eagerly. "Oh, awesome! Give me some fast, Mom. I'm starving," he said with a grin, his earlier fatigue melting away at the prospect of dinner.

His mother laughed softly, seeing the sudden burst of excitement in her son. “Alright, alright, hold your horses,” she said, standing up and heading toward the kitchen. She returned with a plate of steaming spaghetti, the garlic bread still warm and crisp on the side.

She set the plate in front of him with a smile. “Here you go, champ. Eat up. You’ll need all the energy for tomorrow.”

Arwin wasted no time, digging in as the rich flavors of the meal filled his senses. For a moment, all the thoughts of Mars, cricket, and his looming decision disappeared, replaced by the simple joy of his favorite dish.

As Arwin finished his dinner, leaning back in his chair with a satisfied sigh, his parents exchanged a quick glance, noticing the weariness in his posture. His father turned to him, concern lining his voice.

“You’ve had a long day, Arwin,” his father said, his tone gentle but firm."You should rest now."

His mother chimed in, nodding in agreement. “Your father’s right. You’ve worked hard today, and you’ll need your energy for tomorrow’s game. Why don’t you go to your room and get some sleep?”

Arwin hesitated for a moment, glancing at the clock. He still felt that familiar tug toward the book he’d taken from the library earlier, the one waiting for him on his bedside table, filled with thoughts of space and the mysteries of the universe. But his body was tired, his muscles aching from the long practice, and the weight of the day seemed to press down on him more now that his stomach was full.

He nodded slowly. “Yeah, you’re probably right,” he admitted. “I’ll go rest.”

His parents smiled, pleased with his response. “Good,” his father said. “Get some sleep, and you’ll be ready for tomorrow’s match.”

Arwin stood up from the table, feeling the pull of exhaustion settle over him as he made his way toward his room. Even though his mind was still buzzing with thoughts of Mars and the decisions he'd face tomorrow, the need for rest was undeniable.

"I'll see you in the morning," he called back, giving his parents a small wave as he headed to his room, his steps slower now, heavy with the fatigue of the day.

After a quick shower, Arwin changed out of his cricket whites and into his comfortable night suit, Arwin settled onto his bed, the soft sheets inviting him to relax.

"I'll read the book tomorrow," he murmured to himself, a yawn escaping as he nestled deeper into the pillows. He had every intention of diving into the stories of space exploration and the wonders of the universe, but tonight, he was simply too tired.

With that thought lingering in his mind, he closed his eyes, feeling the heaviness of sleep begin to take hold. As he drifted off, the anticipation of tomorrow lingered just beneath the surface, promising a new chapter in his life, one where he could finally focus on his true passion.

"Goodnight, Mars," he whispered softly, and with that, he surrendered to the comforting darkness of sleep.

III

Arwin awoke early the next morning, sunlight streaming through his bedroom window and casting a warm glow over his room. His heart raced with anticipation, the remnants of sleep quickly fading as the memory of the book flooded back to him. He sat up in bed, glanced at the clock on his nightstand, realizing he had the entire morning free. Today was different—he didn't have to rush off to school. Instead, the excitement of the upcoming cricket match filled the air with a palpable sense of anticipation. The match was set to start at 12 PM, and with that thought, a wave of relief washed over him.

He could spend the morning doing what he loved most—reading about Mars and dreaming of adventures beyond Earth. With no schoolwork or classes to worry about, he felt a sense of freedom he hadn't experienced in a while.

I can finally read about Mars, he thought, already feeling the thrill of discovery tugging at his mind. He swung his legs over the side of the bed and padded across the floor to where he had left the book on his desk.

With a sense of urgency, he opened the book and flipped through the pages until he found the section dedicated to

Mars exploration. His eyes widened as he read about the ambitious plans for human missions to the Red Planet, the technology being developed, and the challenges that lay ahead. Each word ignited his imagination, filling him with dreams of stepping onto Martian soil, of exploring a new world, and of being part of something monumental.

He read about the timeline for future missions, the preparations scientists were making, and the hope that humans would set foot on Mars within the next decade.

Hours passed as he devoured the information, his passion for space reigniting with each line he read. The book painted a vivid picture of what life could be like on Mars—the dusty landscapes, the thin atmosphere, and the thrill of discovery.

After immersing himself in the fascinating details about Mars, Arwin checked the time again. He still had plenty of time before the match. He thought about Kelvin and how much he would appreciate sharing his thoughts about space exploration. They often dreamed together about adventures beyond their small town, and today felt like the perfect opportunity to chat.

With a sense of purpose, Arwin stood up from his bed and headed toward his parents' room. His mom had left her phone charging on the bedside table, and he knew she wouldn't mind him borrowing it for a quick call.

He tiptoed into the room, careful not to disturb his parents, who were still sleeping. The soft morning light filtered through the curtains, casting a peaceful glow around the room. Arwin's heart raced with excitement at the thought of talking to Kelvin about their dreams of space travel.

He spotted his mother's phone and picked it up gently, cradling it in his hands.

After grabbing his mother's phone, Arwin hurried back to his room, a sense of excitement bubbling within him. He wanted to call Kelvin to discuss his thoughts about Mars.

As he entered his room, he placed the phone on his desk and began searching for the piece of paper where he had written down Kelvin's phone number. He rifled through various stacks of papers, notebooks, and books scattered across his desk.

"Where is that number?" he muttered to himself, feeling a twinge of frustration as he pulled out crumpled papers and moved aside his school supplies.

After a moment of searching, he finally spotted a small piece of paper tucked beneath a math textbook. He pulled it out, feeling a rush of relief as he unfolded it. Scanning the notes, his heart raced as he found it—Kelvin's phone number, written in a hurried but familiar handwriting.

"Yes! There it is!" he exclaimed, a grin spreading across his face.

With the number in hand, he took a deep breath, excitement coursing through him. He couldn't wait to call Kelvin and dive into their conversation about cricket and their shared dreams of space exploration.

Arwin dialed the number, anticipation bubbling up as he waited for Kelvin to pick up.

After a few rings, Arwin heard the line click, but it was followed by a soft, muffled sound. "Hello?" came Kelvin's voice, thick with sleep and barely audible.

"Hey, Kelvin! It's Arwin!" he said, trying to sound cheerful. "Sorry if I woke you up. I didn't check the time!"

There was a moment of silence before Kelvin replied, his voice a bit clearer now. "Oh, hey! No problem. I was just napping. What's up?"

I have to tell you about some incredible stuff I read about Mars in that book we borrowed from the library!"

"Mars?" Kelvin's interest piqued, the sleepiness in his voice fading. "What about Mars?"

"The book mentioned that scientists are planning missions to Mars within the next decade. Can you believe it? They're talking about sending humans there as early as the 2040s!"

"Really?" Kelvin replied, his excitement evident. "What's the plan? Are they just going to hop on a spaceship and fly there?"

"Kind of!" Arwin responded, feeling the rush of excitement. "They're working on building spacecraft that can carry astronauts to Mars. The journey will take about six to nine months, depending on how they plan the trip. But once they get there, it's not just about landing and taking pictures. They want to set up bases to explore and study the planet!"

"Bases? Like little cities on Mars?" Kelvin asked, his imagination running wild.

"Exactly!" Arwin said, his enthusiasm bubbling over. "They'll create habitats where astronauts can live and work. They're even figuring out how to use Martian soil to grow food and generate oxygen. It's a huge step for humanity!"

"One day we could be part of that journey, Kelvin! Imagine being one of the first explorers on Mars, discovering its secrets and making history!"

"Yeah! I can picture it now: Arwin and Kelvin, Martian explorers!" Kelvin laughed, his eyes brightening with excitement. "We'll be famous! Everyone will want our autographs!"

Arwin chuckled along, feeling a warmth in his chest. "Exactly! We'll tell everyone how we trained hard and dreamed big. And when we stand on that red planet, we'll know that we made it happen."

Kelvin asked, his voice filled with curiosity. "What else did you learn about Mars?"

"Oh, there's so much more!" Arwin replied, his excitement reigniting. "Did you know Mars has the largest dust storms in the solar system? They can cover the entire planet and last for weeks! It's like a massive sandstorm that can be seen from space."

"Wow, that sounds intense!" Kelvin exclaimed. "But how do they survive that?"

"Good question! The spacecraft and habitats they're designing have to withstand those storms. They'll have to be really sturdy," Arwin explained. "Plus, the astronauts will need to stay inside during the worst of it. It's all about safety and preparation."

Kelvin nodded, captivated. "And what about the temperature? Is it freezing there?"

"Yeah, it gets super cold—like, minus 80 degrees Fahrenheit at night!" Arwin said, shivering at the thought. "But during the day, it can get surprisingly warm, around 70 degrees Fahrenheit near the equator. The temperature swings are wild!"

"That's insane! So, they'll have to wear special suits all the time?" Kelvin asked, imagining the futuristic gear.

"Exactly! The suits are designed to protect them from the cold and the thin atmosphere," Arwin explained. "And speaking of atmosphere, Mars has about 1% of Earth's atmosphere, which is why it's so hard for humans to breathe there. That's why they're working on systems to create breathable air in the habitats."

"Man, it sounds like they have a lot to figure out," Kelvin said, shaking his head in disbelief. "But it's kind of amazing that they're actually working on it."

"I know! And here's the coolest part," Arwin said, his voice dropping to a whisper, as if sharing a secret. "Mars has two moons, Phobos and Deimos. They're tiny and look kind of like potatoes! Imagine watching the sunset with those two moons in the sky. It must be beautiful!"

We should start calling ourselves 'Martian explorers' now!" Kelvin laughed, clearly caught up in the excitement.

"Definitely! And there's so much more to learn! The more I read, the more I want to know," Arwin replied, feeling a spark of determination. "I can't wait to dive into more books about space and Mars. Who knows what else we'll discover?"

"Anything else you learned?" Kelvin prompted, his voice still brimming with curiosity.

"Yeah! One of the most fascinating things is that Mars used to have water flowing on its surface. There are signs of ancient rivers and lakes, which means it might have been capable of supporting life long ago," Arwin explained, his eyes lighting up. "Imagine what it must have been like!"

"Wait, really? So there could have been living things on Mars at some point?" Kelvin asked, astonished.

"Exactly! Scientists believe that if life ever existed, it could have been microbial. They're trying to find evidence of that with the rovers exploring the planet right now," Arwin replied, his mind racing with the possibilities. "That's why exploring Mars is so important; if we can find signs of past life, it would change everything we know about life in the universe!"

Kelvin nodded, his expression serious. "That's kind of mind-blowing. It makes you think about our place in the universe. If there was life on Mars, what else is out there?"

"Right? It makes the idea of going to Mars feel even more significant. It's not just about exploration; it's about understanding who we are and where we came from," Arwin said, his voice filled with passion. "If we can uncover the mysteries of Mars, we might learn more about Earth, too."

"Wow, that's deep, Arwin. I never thought about it that way," Kelvin replied, visibly impressed. "So, when we become Martian explorers, we'll be part of something bigger—a quest for knowledge!"

"Exactly! It's like we're on the edge of a new frontier. And if we can contribute to that in any way, it would be incredible," Arwin said, his heart racing at the thought. "Plus, it's our chance to inspire others, just like how we're inspired by those who came before us."

"Yeah! We could be the ones to motivate the next generation of explorers," Kelvin said enthusiastically. "It's like we're part of a legacy, paving the way for future adventures!"

Arwin couldn't help but smile. "And just think about all the stories we'll have to tell! We'll be able to share our journey, the challenges we faced, and how we overcame them. It'll be epic!"

"Totally! I can see it now: kids will gather around us, wide-eyed, as we recount our adventures on Mars. We'll be legends!" Kelvin laughed, and Arwin joined in, their shared excitement filling the air.

"Kelvin," Arwin began, hesitating for a moment. "I've been thinking a lot about something lately. I think... I think I need to quit cricket."

The line went quiet for a moment before Kelvin's voice returned, slightly surprised. "Quit cricket? Really? What brought this on?"

Arwin took a deep breath, letting his thoughts spill out. "I don't know. I just don't feel excited about it anymore. I've been so caught up with everything we've been talking about—space, Mars, black holes... all of it. I want to focus on that. I mean, I want to be the first person on Mars. And to do that, I can't spend all my time on cricket. I need to focus on studying."

Kelvin was quiet for a moment, thinking it over. Then, he spoke, his voice thoughtful. "Yeah... I get it. Honestly, I've noticed you've been distracted during practice lately. I think you're right— you're serious about going to Mars, you can't really focus on both cricket and science. It's too much. You should focus on what really drives you."

Arwin felt a rush of relief hearing his friend say that. "You think so? I mean, I've been feeling guilty about it, like I'm letting everyone down."

"No way," Kelvin replied firmly. "You're not letting anyone down. You're choosing what's important to you. And it's not like you're just quitting for no reason—you're going after something huge. Being the first human on Mars? That's way bigger than cricket."

A smile crept onto Arwin's face. "Thanks, Kelvin. I really needed to hear that. I was planning to talk to my parents today."

"You should," Kelvin encouraged. "They'll be proud. And honestly, it's better to focus on one thing than split your attention between two things you're not fully into. You're passionate about space, man. Go for it."

Arwin nodded, feeling lighter already. Arwin said, his excitement rising. "There's so much out there that we don't understand yet. And I want to be part of discovering it. Cricket just doesn't compare to that."

I was also reading about black holes in that book we borrowed from the library, and it's mind-blowing!" Arwin exclaimed, his excitement bubbling over.

"Black holes? Like, the ones that suck everything in?" Kelvin asked, now fully alert.

"Exactly! They're these massive regions in space where gravity is so strong that nothing, not even light, can escape. It's wild to think about!" Arwin said, the words tumbling out as he remembered the facts he had read. "When a massive star runs out of fuel, it collapses under its own gravity, and if it's heavy enough, it becomes a black hole."

"Wow! So, they start as stars? That's crazy," Kelvin replied, trying to wrap his mind around the concept. "And there are different types, right?"

"Yes! There are stellar black holes, which are a few times the mass of our sun, and then there are supermassive black holes, which can be millions or even billions of times heavier! Like the one at the center of our galaxy, Sagittarius A*," Arwin explained, feeling the thrill of sharing knowledge with his best friend.

"I read about that one too!" Kelvin said, his voice filled with enthusiasm. "It's amazing how they can influence everything around them. I learned about the event horizon—the point of no return!"

"Exactly! Once you cross it, you're gone—sucked into the black hole forever!" Arwin continued, lowering his voice as if revealing a secret.

"Terrifying! But also kind of cool. Can you imagine being near one? What would it look like?"

"I read that black holes are invisible because no light can escape, but you can see their effects on nearby stars and gas. They create these swirling disks called accretion disks, and they can get super hot and emit X-rays," Arwin explained, picturing the swirling colors in his mind. "And when they merge, they create gravitational waves—ripples in spacetime!"

"Whoa, that's like something out of a movie!" Kelvin said, his imagination igniting. "Do you think we'll ever be able to travel to one? I'd love to see one up close, even if it's just a hologram."

"I hope so! And imagine if we could figure out how to harness that gravity or use black holes for time travel," Arwin mused, his thoughts racing. "I mean, scientists are still trying to understand how they work, especially the whole information paradox—how information can get lost when something falls in."

"Information paradox? That sounds deep. What's that about?" Kelvin asked, intrigued.

"It's the idea that if something goes into a black hole, all the information about it disappears, which contradicts quantum mechanics. It's like a cosmic mystery!" Arwin said, feeling a sense of wonder. "It makes me think about how much we still don't know about the universe."

As Arwin continued to share his excitement about Mars, a voice echoed from the background. "Kelvin, get ready for school! You'll be late!" His mother's voice came through the phone, a reminder that time was slipping away.

"Yeah, I know, Mom!" Kelvin replied, glancing at the clock and feeling the urgency settle in. "I'll call you back later, Arwin," he said, trying to sound casual but unable to hide his reluctance to end the conversation.

"No problem! Just make sure you tell me all about your day when we talk again!" Arwin responded, a hint of understanding in his voice.

As they ended the call, Arwin felt a surge of hope and inspiration. The thought of exploring Mars with Kelvin by his side fueled his dreams, reminding him that their friendship could take them anywhere—even to the stars.

Arwin left his room, the echoes of his phone conversation with Kelvin still lingering in his mind. As he walked down the hallway, the sounds of a typical morning drifted through the house—the gentle clink of dishes, the low hum of his parents talking, and the smell of freshly brewed coffee filling the air.

When he entered the kitchen, he found his mother standing by the stove, her back turned as she prepared breakfast, while his father sat at the dining table, flipping through the morning newspaper. The scene felt calm and routine, yet Arwin's mind was anything but. The mysteries of black holes, Mars, and the universe swirled in his head, making his upcoming cricket match feel almost trivial.

"Good morning!" Arwin called out, his voice bright but with a hint of distraction.

His mother turned, smiling warmly. "Good morning, sweetheart," she replied, her voice soft. "Breakfast will be ready soon. How did you sleep?"

"Pretty well," Arwin said, though sleep had come only after his thoughts had finally quieted down late into the night. He walked over to the dining table and slid into a chair across from his father, who lowered the newspaper just enough to glance over the top.

"Morning, son," his father greeted him, a nod of approval in his voice. "Big day today, huh? Your match is at noon?"

Arwin nodded but hesitated for a second, his mind clearly elsewhere. "Yeah, it's at noon." He fiddled with the edge of the tablecloth, trying to muster some enthusiasm.

"Arwin! Go freshen up, breakfast is ready!" his mom's voice echoed from the kitchen, pulling him from his thoughts.

With a sigh, Arwin dragged himself to the washroom. The cold splash of water against his face was refreshing, but it didn't wash away the jumble of thoughts swirling in his mind. Today felt different. He wasn't just thinking about the match—he was thinking about leaving cricket behind for good.

When he returned to the dining room, the smell of breakfast—eggs, toast, and freshly brewed coffee—greeted him. His stomach growled, though his mind was elsewhere.

"Quiet today, aren't you?" his mom said as she placed a plate in front of him.

Arwin gave a half-hearted smile, picking at his food. "Just thinking."

His father folded his newspaper and glanced over. "Thinking about the big match? Big day for you, son."

Arwin paused, then nodded, though the match was the last thing on his mind. "Yeah, something like that."

As he ate, his thoughts kept drifting to Mars. The book he'd read that morning had reignited his passion. Space, black holes, Mars—it all felt so much more important than the cricket match. He quickly finished his breakfast, not even tasting the food as he downed it in record time.

"Done already?" his mom asked, raising an eyebrow. "You barely took a breath!"

"Yeah, just got a lot on my mind," he said, pushing his chair back and heading to his room to change.

Standing in front of his wardrobe, Arwin pulled out his cricket kit—a pristine white uniform. Normally, it filled him with pride, but today, it felt oddly out of place, like wearing an old costume that didn't fit anymore. He hesitated for a moment, staring at it, before finally slipping it on.

As he walked back to the living room, his parents were waiting by the door, smiles on their faces.

"Good luck today," his mom said, ruffling his hair. "You've trained hard, and whatever happens, we're proud of you."

Arwin forced a smile, appreciating their support, but he couldn't shake the feeling that soon, everything was going to change.

"Thanks," he said, his voice quieter than usual. "I'll do my best."

He slung his cricket bag over his shoulder, feeling its weight heavier than ever. As he stepped outside, a breeze hit him, and he took a deep breath. The world seemed to slow down for a moment, as if it, too, knew something was shifting.

This was the last time he'd be playing cricket, and while it should've made him feel sad or nostalgic, all he could think about was Mars, the stars, and what lay beyond.

With one last glance at his parents, he headed toward the field, knowing that soon, he'd have to tell them about his decision. But for now, there was one last game to play.

As Arwin reached the cricket ground, the familiar buzz of excitement filled the air. Both teams were already warming up—some players were jogging along the boundary, while others were practicing their catches.

His teammates waved him over, and he joined them for some light stretching and throwing practice. Normally, this would have him fired up, but his mind was elsewhere. His thoughts kept drifting back to Mars, to the vastness of space and all the possibilities it held.

Suddenly, the captain of his team called out, "Arwin! It's time for the toss!"

Arwin snapped out of his thoughts and jogged over to the center of the field where the two captains stood with the umpire.

The coin landed with a soft thud on the pitch. His team had won the toss.

“We’ll ball first,” his captain said confidently, and the rest of the team nodded in agreement.

As everyone prepared for the start of the match, Arwin glanced around the field. The cheers, the energy, the camaraderie—it all felt surreal today.

After a brief huddle, the fielders took their positions on the field. The captain, with a serious look on his face, began directing the players, adjusting positions with sharp hand signals. "Arwin, deep mid-wicket!" he shouted, and Arwin jogged to his spot.

As fielders settled into position, the openers from the opposing team walked confidently to the crease, bats in hand. The tension in the air was palpable, a familiar pre-match feeling, but Arwin couldn’t shake the sense that this moment wasn’t as important as it used to feel. The openers did a few practice swings, and the umpire called for the start of play.

The bowler stood at the top of his run-up, eyes locked onto the batsman. The field was set, the tension thick in the air.

With a final glance at the batsman, the bowler surged forward, his feet pounding against the grass in a rhythmic cadence. As he reached the crease, he delivered the first ball of the innings with a flick of his wrist, sending the leather ball hurtling through the air like a missile.

The batsman, a seasoned player with years of experience, watched the ball’s trajectory intently. He crouched slightly, his bat raised, ready to respond. As the ball neared, he swung his bat down with precision, executing a perfectly timed defensive stroke.

The impact echoed through the ground—a sharp thwack as the ball met the bat, before it dribbled gently back to the bowler. The batsman stood firm, unyielding, demonstrating his control and skill, while the bowler grimaced slightly, knowing he'd need to bring more to the table to break through.

The cricket match was in full swing, but Arwin felt like something was off. He wasn't playing like he used to. His teammates were giving it their all, but Arwin's mind was elsewhere.

"Just for today," Arwin muttered to himself, squatting slightly as he took his position in the field. The sun beat down on him, casting long shadows across the grass. He could hear the chatter of his teammates nearby, the distant laughter of friends, but his mind was miles away.

He felt a mix of excitement and trepidation, cricket had always been a part of him, but now it felt like a chapter closing.

"I will not continue cricket anymore," he said softly, almost like a vow. The words hung in the air around him, weighty and irrevocable. There was a time when the sound of the ball hitting the bat had filled him with joy, but now, that joy was overshadowed by a burning passion for something else. Space, science, and the endless possibilities of the universe had ignited a fire in him that cricket could no longer match.

No more distractions, he told himself, watching as the bowler prepared for another delivery. I need to focus on what truly matters now.

The ball arched gracefully, a white comet against the backdrop of blue. Time seemed to slow as it descended, gravity pulling it back to the earth. The crowd held its breath, their eyes following the trajectory.

Just then, the shout of a teammate broke through his reverie. "Arwin! Catch it!"

The ball flew high into the air, right toward him, but Arwin barely moved.

A collective gasp rippled through the crowd as the ball hit the ground with a dull thud, bouncing away from him. Arwin's heart sank, disappointment flooding his chest. His teammates exchanged glances, a mix of concern and frustration etched on their faces.

"Arwin! What are you doing?" the captain shouted, his voice tense. "You're one of our best players! If you don't focus, we're going to lose this game!"

Arwin snapped back to reality. "Sorry, it won't happen again," he said, but he wasn't sure he believed it himself.

It was the last ball of the innings, and the pressure was building. The team had scored 150 runs in 20 overs, and now it was up to Arwin to finish strong. He took a deep breath, his heart pounding in his chest, and stepped up to bat. He could feel everyone's eyes on him.

As the innings progressed, Arwin felt the familiar rush of adrenaline as he walked toward the crease, his heart pounding in rhythm with the chants of his teammates.

"Arwin! You can do this! You've got this!" they shouted, their voices a blend of encouragement and excitement.

It was a moment that should have filled him with joy, yet a strange tension hung in the air. He stepped up to the crease, gripping the bat tightly. The bowler eyed him with determination, the ball glinting under the sunlight like a small planet ready to be launched into orbit. But as Arwin settled into his stance, the cheers of his teammates faded into the background, replaced by the sound of his own heartbeat. I can do this, he told himself, but the words felt hollow, like an echo in a vast, empty space. He glanced at his friends, their faces filled with anticipation.

The bowler rushed in, and Arwin swung hard.

Arwin stepped onto the pitch, the weight of his cricket bat feeling comforting in his hands. He glanced at his opening partner, Sam, who grinned back at him, his eyes sparkling with enthusiasm. Together, they walked toward the crease, feeling the thrill of the moment pulse through them.

As they took their positions, Arwin could hear the supportive chatter of his teammates behind him and the murmurs of the crowd, a sea of faces eager to see what they would do next. The bowler stood at the other end, eyeing them with determination, but Arwin felt a surge of confidence wash over him. They had a score to chase, and he was ready to contribute.

The bowler began his run-up, and Arwin settled into his stance, eyes locked on the approaching ball. With a swift motion, the bowler released it, the ball came at him like a bullet, but Arwin was ready. He swung his bat with precision, making solid contact. The ball rocketed off the edge of his bat, soaring toward the boundary. Cheers erupted from the crowd as it raced across the grass, landing just shy of the boundary line and rolling away.

"Four runs!" someone shouted from the sidelines, and Arwin felt a rush of exhilaration as he and Sam exchanged high-fives.

"Great start!" Sam grinned, his excitement palpable.

With renewed energy, they continued their innings, each ball faced turning into a small victory. Arwin found himself settling into a rhythm, working in tandem with Sam, rotating the strike, and picking gaps in the field.

As they reached the halfway Sam, their confidence surged. With each run, the cheers grew louder, and the feeling of camaraderie among the team filled the air.

"Let's keep this going!" Sam encouraged, glancing over at Arwin, who nodded, feeling the weight of their mission.

The runs kept piling up, and they were nearing their target, still with both openers standing firm.

"Just a little more, and we'll do it!" he thought.

The atmosphere at the cricket ground was electric, the crowd on the edge of their seats. With only six runs needed from the final six balls, Arwin could feel the weight of the moment pressing down on him. His heart raced, pounding like a drum in his chest as he faced the bowler, his palms slightly sweaty around the handle of his bat.

"Come on, Arwin! You've got this!" Sam shouted from the other end, his voice filled with encouragement. Arwin glanced at him and saw the determination in his friend's eyes, a reminder that they were in this together.

As the bowler released the ball, time seemed to stretch. Arwin's instincts kicked in; he could see the ball spinning toward him with fierce speed. He took a deep breath, feeling the weight of the moment settle on his shoulders.

With a powerful swing of his bat, Arwin connected with the ball—CRACK! The sound reverberated across the field, a sweet note of success that sent a rush of adrenaline coursing through him. The ball soared into the air, rising higher and higher, leaving the ground behind.

The crowd erupted into a collective roar, their voices blending into a cacophony of excitement. “SIX!” someone shouted, and the word echoed like a chant, fueling Arwin’s exhilaration. He watched as the ball arced gracefully against the blue sky, gliding like a comet streaking through space and then, it hit the ground.

Arwin! You did it!” Sam shouted, his voice ringing out above the din. Arwin’s heart swelled as he saw the pure elation in his friends’ eyes, their smiles wide enough to rival the sun.

Within seconds, they reached him, lifting him off the ground in a whirlwind of excitement. “We won! We won!” they chanted, their voices melding into a joyous chorus.

“Look at you, superstar!” one of his teammates called, his laughter echoing as he playfully tossed Arwin into the air.

As he landed back in their arms, he was engulfed in a group hug. They spun him around, their voices a blur of congratulations and cheers.

His teammates cheered and lifted him onto their shoulders, but instead of feeling proud, Arwin felt nothing. The excitement that usually came with a win wasn’t there. Without a word, Arwin jumped off his friends‘ shoulders and ran all the way home, leaving the celebration behind.

As Arwin walked along the familiar path toward home, the sun dipped below the horizon, casting a warm golden hue across the landscape. His heart raced at the idea of telling his parents.

“They’re going to be so proud,” he thought, envisioning their faces lighting up with excitement. This wasn’t just a dream; it was something monumental. “My parents will love the idea that their son wants to explore the universe!”

Arwin approached the front door and rang the bell, his heart racing with anticipation. A moment later, his mother opened the door, her face lighting up with a warm smile.

"Welcome home, sweetie!" she said, stepping aside to let him in.

He burst through the door, breathing heavily.

"Hey, Arwin! How was the cricket match?" his dad asked from the living room.

"I don't want to be a cricketer anymore!" he shouted to his parents.

His dad looked shocked. "What? Cricket is your passion. You love it more than anything. Why the sudden change?"

Arwin shook his head. "Not anymore. I want to do something different, something bigger. I want to study space. I want to be an astronaut!"

His dad frowned in confusion. "Space? Where is this coming from?"

Arwin's eyes were wide with excitement.

"When Kelvin and I talk about the universe, it excites me so much. I feel like I've been chosen to understand it, to discover what's out there. I want to know why we're here and what lies beyond the stars.

I want to devote my whole life to finding answers to the big questions out there. I want to be an astronaut and explore the universe!" I will go to Mars, explore space, and find out the answers to all those big questions."

His dad stared at him for a moment, trying to take it all in. "Mars? You're serious about this? " Arwin nodded. "Yes, I've never been more sure. Cricket doesn't matter anymore.

I want to see the stars."

His parents stifled their laughter, though they couldn't hide their pride.

"Our seventh grader," his father said with a grin," already thinking like a scientist."

As arwin sat down at the table, he glanced at his mother and asked, "What's for
dinner, Mom?" With a gentle smile, his mother responded, "I made chicken today." But Arwin's
mind was elsewhere.

"Did you hear, Mom? The space agency has announced that they're sending astronauts to Mars."

His parents exchanged amused glances before his father chuckled and said, "Well, if you keep up with your studies and work hard, you just might have a chance to get there."

arwin's mother, ever practical, reminded him, "You should get some rest now. You've got school tomorrow."

Arwin, frowning slightly, responded, "But I don't like going to school."

His mother looked at him thoughtfully and asked, "How do you expect to go to Mars if you don't enjoy school? Why don't you like it?"

With a sigh, Arwin explained, "The way the teachers teach-it's just not interesting. They make us memorize dates and facts, but I don't want to learn all that. I only like talking about space with Kelvin."

He leaned back, his frustration palpable, "I want to understand how the universe works, why it exists. And there's not even an astronomy class in our school."

Arwin's dad glanced at the clock and said, "Alright, future astronaut, it's time to head to bed. School awaits tomorrow. Just remember, whatever path you choose, we'll always be here cheering you on. Follow your passion, and don't be afraid to chase after your dreams."

Arwin felt a rush of affection as he stepped forward and enveloped his father in a warm hug. The embrace felt like a safe harbor, a place where he could find comfort and strength. "I'm really happy, Dad. I feel like I can actually chase my dreams now."

After their heartfelt conversation, Arwin felt a sense of relief and gratitude wash over him. He turned to his parents, their faces radiating warmth and understanding. "Thank you for being so supportive," he said, his voice filled with sincerity. "It means a lot to me that you understand what I want."

His mother smiled brightly, her eyes sparkling with pride. "We'll always be here for you, Arwin. Your happiness is what matters most to us."

Arwin's father nodded in agreement. "Follow your dreams, son. We believe in you."

Feeling buoyed by their encouragement, Arwin gave them both a grateful smile. He turned and made his way down the hallway to his room, the soft carpet beneath his feet comforting him as he walked.

As he entered his room, he paused for a moment, glancing back at his parents. "I really appreciate everything," he said again, his heart swelling with love. Their understanding meant the world to him, and he felt more determined than ever to chase his dreams.

Once inside his room, he closed the door gently and let out a contented sigh. But Arwin wasn't ready for sleep, he sneaked out to the balcony, gazing up at the endless expanse of the night sky. The stars shimmered above him, their light reflected in his wide eyes. His heart raced with excitement. One day, he thought, I'll be up there. I'll find my way to Mars. But for now, he sighed, sleep was inevitable-otherwise, his mother would certainly be furious.

Then he went to bed, Arwin stared up at the ceiling, the soft glow of his bedside lamp casting gentle shadows around the room. His mind was a whirlwind of thoughts, swirling with excitement and gratitude. His father's words echoed in his head: "I want you to be happy always."

That simple statement filled him with warmth. Arwin could feel the weight of his father's unwavering support, like a comforting blanket wrapped around him. He thought about how much his parents believed in him, and it made him realize that he wasn't alone in his journey. They were right there, cheering him on, ready to help him chase his dreams.

With the words of his father echoing softly in his heart, Arwin drifted off to sleep, dreaming of the stars, the endless possibilities ahead, and the promise of a bright tomorrow. In the stillness of the night, he slept soundly, knowing that he had the strength to pursue his dreams and the love of his family to guide him every step of the way.

The next morning, as sunlight crept through the curtains, Arwin groaned when his mother's voice echoed from downstairs.

"Arwin! It's 7 AM! Time for school!" Arwin groaned, pulling the covers over his head.

"Just five more minutes, Mom. Please," he mumbled, trying to steal a few extra moments of sleep,

"You'll be late if you don't get up now," his mother's voice grew firmer. "Get moving!"

Reluctantly, Arwin dragged himself out of bed and stumbled toward the bathroom, his eyes still heavy with sleep. As he stood at the sink, rinsing his hands, his mind began to wander. He stared at the swirling water and mused, "Isn't the sink kind of like a black hole? It pulls in the water, and just like that, it's gone, like it was never there ... Same as a black hole eating up everything around it." He smirked at the thought. He had read all about black holes recently in the space book he had borrowed from the library, and it had sparked a fascination in him.

"Arwin!" his mother's voice pierced through his daydream. "You'll miss the class if you don't hurry!"

"I'm coming!" he called back, shaking off his thoughts as he rushed to get dressed. Downstairs, his mother was already waiting, handing him his packed lunch. "Here, take this. Eat when you can at school," she said, sounding exasperated but warm.

"Thanks, Mom," Arwin replied, distracted as ever, still imagining the vast mysteries of space.

He rushed out the door, but his mind stayed stuck on black holes. He couldn't help but wonder how something so powerful could swallow light, matter-everything. The more he thought about it, the more it felt like the black hole was pulling his thoughts in, too.

When Arwin finally arrived at school, he slipped into his seat just before the bell rang. His classmates were already buzzing with the usual morning chatter. He glanced around the classroom, hoping to catch sight of his friend Kelvin. But as he scanned the room, he realized with a pang of disappointment that Kelvin was absent.

The teacher walked in with a smile and greeted them all, "Good morning, class!"

"Good morning, Miss," everyone replied.

The teacher then scanned the room with an expectant look. "So, who's finished their history homework from yesterday?"

Arwin's heart sank a little as he realized his mind had been so far away in the stars that he had completely forgotten his homework.

Arwin sat at his desk, his mind spinning with worry. How could I forget to do my homework? The thought gnawed at him. His history assignment lay undone, and he knew his teacher wouldn't be pleased.

As the teacher moved around the classroom, checking each student's work one by one, Arwin felt his heart race. He tried to focus on anything else, but his thoughts kept circling back to the inevitable moment when it would be his turn.

The teacher approached, her expression stern as she glanced at the papers of the students before him. Arwin's stomach tightened. And then it came-his turn. The teacher stopped by his desk, looking down at him.

"Arwin, have you done your homework?" she asked, her voice carrying a note of impatience. Arwin swallowed hard and looked up.

"I'm really sorry, Miss. I didn't manage to finish it. I had a cricket match yesterday, and I didn't get the chance to do it."

The teacher's expression shifted from stern to disappointed, her brows knitting together.

"Arwin, this is unacceptable. You need to focus more on your studies. You can't expect to keep up if you don't put in the effort," she admonished, "Cricket or no cricket, excuses won't help you here. I'll have to mark your performance as zero for today."

Arwin's heart sank further. "Please, Miss, don't do that. It won't happen again, I promise! Just give me one more chance."

But his pleading fell on deaf ears. The teacher shook her head, unyielding. "No more chances, Arwin. This is about your responsibility."

Arwin slumped back in his chair, feeling crushed. The teacher's reaction had stung more than he expected. He had hoped for some leniency, but all he felt now was disappointment, not just in himself but also in how coldly the situation had unfolded.

Then lesson begins with the teacher instructing the class to open their textbooks to a specific page, where they were supposed to study the world during Hitler's era.

As Mrs Penrose outlined the rise of the Nazi Party, Arwin's mind drifted. He glanced out the window, watching leaves dance in the breeze, wishing he could be outside exploring instead of stuck in class.

Mrs Penrose began sketching a timeline on the whiteboard, detailing the economic struggles of post-World War I Germany. "Hitler promised a return to greatness," he explained, but Arwin barely registered the words.

The room grew quiet as Mrs Penrose displayed images from the era—propaganda posters, rallies, and haunting photographs from concentration camps. "This was a time of real suffering," he emphasized. "Understanding this history is crucial."

However, the teacher quickly reassures them that they will cover this in the next class, leaving the students with a sense of curiosity and anticipation.

The focus then shifts to the physics class. As the teacher steps into the room,

"Good afternoon, everyone," he said, his voice steady but tinged with fatigue. "Today, we're supposed to dive into Newton's laws of motion."

The students replied with a half-hearted chorus of greetings, some barely lifting their heads. Mr. Caldwell took a deep breath, then continued, "However, let's be real: these laws aren't very important for your exams. So, we'll skip this part."

A collective sigh of relief spread through the room, and Arwin felt a mix of frustration and understanding. The pressure of the upcoming exams had transformed their classroom into a race against the clock, where true learning often took a backseat.

"Instead, let's focus on what you actually need to know," Mr. Caldwell said, pacing the front of the room. "We'll cover the main topics that are likely to appear on the tests. I want you to be prepared."

The teacher makes it clear that the students are expected to learn the three laws by heart for the next class. This direct instruction stirs some restlessness among the students, as the task seems daunting.

Arwin, unable to stay silent, stands up and voices his

opinion. He is visibly frustrated with the idea of merely memorizing the laws without understanding their deeper meaning. In a bold move, he challenges the teacher:

"Sir, Newton wasn't just a name to be memorized. He was one of the greatest scientists of all time. His discoveries aren't meant to be learned like a poem; they're meant to be understood."

The classroom falls quiet, as everyone senses the tension between Arwin and the

teacher. A murmur of agreement starts to spread, and then "Please, sir, don't make physics boring. It's such an intriguing subject!" said Arwin.

The teacher, clearly annoyed, replied sharply, "An eighth-grader is going to tell me how to teach? Get out of my class!"

Arwin, trying to stay calm, responded, "Sir, I respect you and didn't mean to upset you. I only wanted to say that understanding the laws is more important than just memorizing them."

But the teacher, still frustrated, wasn't willing to listen any further. He pointed toward the door, and Arwin had no choice but to leave the room. His classmates watched quietly, some whispering to each other as he walked out. Then bell rang, everyone quickly left for home, but the tension from the argument still lingered.

On his way home, Arwin couldn't stop thinking about what had happened. He felt guilty now, also today his friend Kelvin hadn't come to school, leaving him feeling alone in the class. When he finally got home, the day didn't get any better. His parents were in a bad mood and barely spoke to him. They didn't ask how his day had gone, even though he wished they would. Instead, their cold attitude made Arwin feel even worse.

"What happened at school today?" Arwin's father demanded the moment he walked through the door. His voice was stern, and it was clear that something serious had occurred.

"Your teacher called us about the argument you caused today. How could you speak to your teacher that way? Do you think it's acceptable to challenge him like that? You're too young to know what's best for you or what isn't."

Arwin stood silently, the weight of his father's disappointment bearing down on him.

I want to explore, not just memorize some rules!" Tears rolled down his cheeks as he spoke, the frustration bubbling over.

"You have no right to question how your teacher does his job. You must listen to him, and you have to promise me that this will never happen again," his father continued, his tone growing more insistent with every word.

The pressure of the situation became too much for Arwin, and tears welled up in his eyes. Unable to contain his emotions any longer, he turned and ran toward the main gate, desperate to escape the suffocating atmosphere. His father called after him, her voice filled with both frustration and concern.

"Come back, Arwin! If you don't come back now, you won't get dinner tonight!"

But Arwin didn't stop. His heart heavy with sadness, he ran until he reached a quiet spot near the science museum-

a place he and his family often visited together. There, he sat alone, staring into the distance, feeling a deep sense of loneliness and regret. Arwin sat on the bench, his arms crossed and his eyes fixed on the ground. The weight of his thoughts made him feel restless, but he didn't know how to express
them. Across from him sat a man, quietly observing him. After a few moments, the man spoke up.

"You look troubled, child. What's on your mind?" the man asked, his voice calm and reassuring.
Arwin hesitated, not wanting to talk at first.

"It's nothing," he muttered, glancing away.

The man smiled kindly. "Sometimes when you keep things inside, they weigh you
down even more. It helps to share your thoughts."

Arwin shifted uncomfortably, but the man's words lingered, Eventually, he sighed and gave in.

"I had an argument with my physics teacher today," he began, his voice low but steady. "He was telling us to memorize all these laws-Newton's laws, all of it-but that's not what I want. I love physics, I always have.
But it's not just about learning a bunch of rules for me."

The man nodded, encouraging Arwin to continue.

"Physics is supposed to be about understanding how the universe works," Arwin explained, his frustration growing as he spoke.

"It's not just about knowing what happens-it's about understanding why it happens. But my teacher, he doesn't seem to care about that part. He just wants us to memorize the laws and be done with it, And that's not enough for me."

The man leaned forward slightly, his expression thoughtful.

"I see what you mean. Physics is much more than just the laws-it's about exploring the reasons behind them, isn't it? Arwin's face softened a bit, feeling understood for the first time in a while.

"Exactly," he said, his voice carrying more energy. "I want to know why things work the way they do. I want to ask questions, explore ideas, and understand the bigger picture.

Memorizing laws without knowing why they're important doesn't help me. It's frustrating because I know physics is amazing, but the way it's taught makes it feel ... dull."

The man smiled warmly. "And is there a particular part of physics that excites you more than the rest?"

V

Arwin didn't hesitate. "Astrophysics. I'm fascinated by space-how stars form, what black holes are, how the universe began. And astronomy too! I've been reading about it on my own because they don't teach it in school. I don't understand why they leave out the exciting stuff."

The man's smile deepened, a look of understanding crossing his face.

"So, it's not physics itself that frustrates you-it's the way it's being taught. They're not giving you the freedom to explore the bigger questions, the mysteries that really matter to you."

Arwin nodded, his frustration returning. "Exactly. I think that's why a lot of students don't like studying. They feel like they're just being told to follow rules without understanding why those rules exist. It's like they're missing out on the wonder of it all."

The man leaned back slightly, watching Arwin with a thoughtful expression.

"You remind me of myself when I was your age," he said. "School can be challenging, especially when the only focus seems to be on following rules. But I always believed learning should be about curiosity, about finding answers to the questions you're passionate about."

Arwin's eyes widened. "You really think so?" he asked, feeling a spark of hope. The man smiled.

"Absolutely. What's your name, child?"

"Arwin," he replied quietly.

The man leaned back slightly, studying Arwin for a moment before speaking. "Arwin, have you ever wondered if dreams have a connection to the real world?"

Arwin looked puzzled, his brows furrowing. "I'm not sure," he replied. "I've always thought dreams were just random thoughts or something. Do you think they're connected?"

The man smiled, as if expecting the question. "Yes, I do," he said, his voice steady. "Many scientists have different views on dreams. Some say they're just the brain organizing memories, others think they're just meaningless. But I believe they're much more than that. I think dreams are a way for us to connect with something beyond this world."

Arwin leaned in, intrigued. "Something beyond? Like what?"

The man's eyes gleamed with quiet excitement.

"I believe there are higher dimensions-realities that we can't normally see or understand. These dimensions, in my view, communicate with us through dreams. When we dream, we're not just replaying the day's events or processing our thoughts. We're tapping into something greater, something that exists beyond the limits of our understanding."

Arwin's mind raced with possibilities. "So, you think dreams are more than just random thoughts-they're messages? From other dimensions?"

The man nodded. "Yes. Dreams are like a bridge between us and those higher realities. They can show us things we're meant to see, guide us toward something important, or even help us understand things that our waking mind can't comprehend. If you pay close attention, dreams can offer glimpses into truths we
aren't aware of when we're awake."

Arwin sat back, absorbing the man's words. "I've never thought of dreams like that," he admitted. "It's like they're trying to tell us something, but we just don't know how to listen."
The man smiled softly. "Exactly. Dreams are more powerful than we give them credit for. They're a way for those higher dimensions to communicate with us, to share knowledge and insight, if only we're willing to listen."

Arwin hesitated. "Well ... is that real? Can it really happen?"

The man's smile grew wider. "Everything is possible in this universe, Arwin. The universe is a very interesting place, filled with mysteries we've barely begun to understand. The connection between dreams and higher dimensions might be one of those mysteries."

Arwin's whole outlook shifted with this conversation. He had never thought about dreams in such a way before. This talk left him both amazed and excited. He felt a sense of joy growing inside him, especially seeing that an adult could talk about something as fascinating as space and dreams. After a moment of silence, Arwin asked, "Do you also like astrophysics?"

The man smiled again and said, "Yes, a lot."

"My dream is to be the first to lead a human mission to Mars. I want to go there and never turn back," Arwin declared with a mix of determination and excitement.

The old man raised an eyebrow, seemingly intrigued. "Nice. You're making my day, boy," he remarked softly. "But what if I want to show you something?"
Arwin hesitated, staring at the man, unsure of what to make of the unexpected offer. "Show me something? What do you mean?" he asked, his voice tinged with both curiosity and caution.
The man tilted his head thoughtfully, as if weighing his words. "If you came with me, you'd find out," he said, his tone calm, almost nonchalant.

Arwin's mind raced. He knew it would be reckless to follow a stranger without knowing what lay ahead. Yet, something in the man's demeanor made him pause.

Was it safe? Could he trust him?

"Can't you show me here?" Arwin asked, still trying to gauge the situation. The man shook his head slowly. "It's not that simple. What I want to show you is ... well, it's big," he said, his eyes glinting with a hint of mystery.

Silence stretched between them, Arwin's instincts warned

him to turn away, but his curiosity was growing stronger by the second. He could sense that the man wasn't lying-or if he was, he was doing a very good job of hiding it.

"Okay," Arwin murmured, weighing the risk against the possibility. "Show me."

The man nodded slowly, a faint smile tugging at his lips. "Alright, boy. Follow me." Arwin took a deep breath and stepped forward. There was no turning back now.

He would follow this man-this stranger-into the unknown, hoping to uncover whatever it was that couldn't be explained in words.

The two began walking in silence, the man leading Arwin down unfamiliar streets. He was cautious but couldn't shake the sense that he was safe. Something about the man's calm, intelligent demeanor reassured him.

"Where are we going?" he finally managed to ask, his voice barely above a whisper.

"Just a little further," the man replied, his tone steady but uninformative.

Arwin's heart raced. Thoughts of the familiar neighborhood—the laughter of friends, the warmth of family—flooded his mind, and he felt a tightness in his chest.

When they arrived at the man's house, the front door opened almost immediately. A woman stood in the doorway, her expression warm and welcoming. "Good evening," Arwin said, a little nervous. The woman smiled at him.

"Good evening. And what's your name, young man?"

"Arwin," he replied, feeling slightly more comfortable.

The man stepped forward and explained to his wife, "This is Arwin. He's a smart kid, but he's got some big ideas. He's not too fond of the education system either."

The wife's eyes widened, her face breaking into an impressed smile. "That's great," she said,
glancing at her husband. "Where did you find him?" The man began explaining the circumstances under which they met, recounting their earlier conversation.

As the words flowed, Arwin suddenly realized something-they had been talking for quite a while, and yet he still didn't know the man's name.

The man smiled, extending his hand.

"Dr. James Carter."

Arwin blinked, the name ringing in his ears. Dr. James Carter? He stared, wide-eyed and shocked. Could it really be the James Carter-the renowned scientist who had made groundbreaking discoveries in space
exploration? Arwin had read about him countless times in science magazines. And here he was, standing right in front of him.

"The James Carter?" Arwin asked, his voice barely a whisper. Dr. Carter chuckled. "The one and only." Arwin felt a rush of excitement and awe flood through him. "That explains why talking with you felt ... different," he muttered, trying to keep his composure but utterly starstruck.

Arwin felt his heart leap in excitement and disbelief. His admiration for the
man standing before him grew tenfold. "That explains a lot," he murmured, still in awe. "Talking to you felt different."

Dr. Carter's eyes twinkled as he acknowledged the boy's comment. "I'm glad it did. You've got an impressive way of thinking for your age, Arwin. Physics can be understood-even by someone as young as you.

Arwin beamed at the praise, nodding enthusiastically.

"Thank you, Dr. Carter. I always believed that too."

Dr. Carter's tone grew more serious as he inquired, "But tell me, Arwin, have you informed your parents that you're with me?"

Arwin's face flushed, his stomach flipping. "Oh no," he stammered, realizing his mistake. In the excitement of the day, it had completely slipped his mind.

I forgot to tell them," he confessed, shaking his head, disappointed in himself. "I got caught up in everything." Dr. Carter offered a sympathetic nod. "It's understandable. But it's important they know where you are. Relieved at Dr. Carter's understanding, Arwin nodded and gratefully accepted the phone that Dr.Carter handed him.

He quickly dialed his home number, his heart racing as he waited for the line to pick up. After a few rings, his mother's familiar voice answered.

Her voice was sharp with worry and anger. "Arwin, where are you? We've been frantic! How could you just disappear like this?"

He hesitated. "I'm at James Carter's house. He met me near the Science Museum."

"James Carter?" she repeated, incredulous. "Why would he-" Before she could finish, Arwin heard his father shouting in the background. "Is that him? Where is he?"

His father's voice grew louder until he grabbed the phone. "You listen to me, Arwin. You come home now, or don't bother coming back! I won't let you in if you don't walk through that door in the next hour."

"Dad, please," Arwin pleaded, his chest tightening. "Just give me some time. I'll be back, I swear."

But the line went dead, his father's threat hanging heavily in the silence. Arwin stared at the phone, frozen.

"What happened, Arwin? James asked, his voice firm but gentle. Arwin hesitated, shifting nervously. His eyes avoided James as he replied,

"I left the house after the argument ... It all started because of the teachers ... " His voice trailed off, as if he wasn't sure how to explain further.

James frowned, sensing that Arwin wasn't telling the full story. "You shouldn't have done that," he said seriously. "You should have told your parents. This isn't something to keep from them. Promise me you won't do this again."

Arwin looked down, his shoulders slumping. "I promise," he muttered, though there was doubt in his voice."

I won't do it again.

Just then, James' wife, who had been listening, suggested, "James, why don't you show him the basement? He might find it fascinating. Then, send him home since his parents are waiting."

James nodded. "Come on, Arwin. There's something cool I want to show you."

They descended the stairs into the basement, which led to a nice, dark space that felt cozy and inviting. As they reached the bottom, In the center of the room, a sturdy table was cluttered with beakers, flasks, and a polished microscope, ready for experiments. A stunning model of the solar system hung from the ceiling, each planet rotating slowly, captivating the eye.

Against one wall stood two astronaut suits, meticulously arranged and gleaming under the soft light. James proudly gestured toward them. "These are the suits I've been working on. With these, you can go to Mars!"

A telescope pointed toward a small window, surrounded by star charts and notebooks filled with observations. The basement felt like a portal to another world, its sturdy wooden beams overhead echoing with the whispers of past experiments and dreams. Stacks of notebooks filled with sketches and calculations teetered precariously on every available surface, while a chalkboard covered in equations and diagrams revealed the ambitious thoughts of its young inventor.

A corner was dedicated to a small collection of robotics parts, their metallic surfaces glinting in the soft light, hinting at projects yet to be realized. The walls were adorned with posters of astronauts and spacecraft, fueling the imagination with visions of exploration beyond Earth. A vintage globe sat on a side table, its faded colors suggesting countless adventures waiting to be charted. In this cluttered sanctuary, creativity thrived, and the potential for discovery hung in the air like a promise. The basement was a hub of imagination and science, where dreams of exploration and adventure awaited.

Arwin stood in the dim light of the basement, a sense of joy swelling within him as he immersed himself in his thoughts. The space, filled with books and old equipment, felt like a treasure trove of potential, igniting a motivation he hadn't experienced in ages. The atmosphere buzzed with the promise of
discovery, and he couldn't help but smile. James, observing Arwin's uplifted spirit, leaned against a nearby
workbench, a knowing glint in his eye.

"You seem different, Arwin," he remarked, breaking the comfortable silence.

"You know, that light up there -" he gestured to the overhead bulb, flickering slightly, "-it carries energy."

Arwin turned his gaze to the flickering light, intrigued yet puzzled. "Light?" he echoed, curiosity piquing his interest.

James nodded eagerly. "Light is made of photons. They carry energy. If we could figure out how to convert that energy into mass, we might be able to see the past or even the future."

Arwin's eyes widened in shock, his earlier happiness giving way to disbelief. "How?" he asked, his voice tinged with a mix of excitement and confusion.

"Photons don't experience time," James explained, leaning closer, his enthusiasm contagious. "They travel at the speed of light, which means that for them, time doesn't pass. If we could harness that energy and turn it into something tangible, we might unlock the ability to look beyond our current understanding of time."

Arwin's excitement froze mid-smile. His face tightened, eyes widening in shock as he stared out the window. The light, once soft and warm, now seemed to carry a strange weight.

As the warm glow of the overhead light began to dim with the setting sun, a sense of urgency crept into the basement. James glanced at Arwin, noting how lost he seemed in his thoughts, his gaze still fixated on the flickering bulb as if it held the secrets of the universe.

"Arwin," James said gently, breaking the spell of silence,

"you should head out now. It's getting late."

He leaned back against the workbench, a hint of reluctance in his voice. "We can pick this up next time."

But Arwin barely heard him. His mind was still racing through a realm where everything was possible-where photons could unlock doors to the past and future, where the ordinary light overhead held the potential for extraordinary discoveries. The basement felt like a launchpad to uncharted territories of knowledge and imagination.

Finally, Arwin blinked and slowly returned to the present, the realization hitting him.

"Oh, right. I guess I should."

But even as he spoke, he lingered, still entranced by the possibilities dancing in his mind. The weight of potential hung in the air, urging him to stay just a little longer, to explore just a bit more.

"See you soon, Dr James," he said, a soft smile creeping across his face, as he turned to leave, his heart racing with the thrill of discovery and the tantalizing thought that anything could happen next time they met.

As Arwin stepped out of the basement, he was greeted by Mrs. Carter, the kind, elderly woman who lived in the apartment upstairs. She was tending to her potted plants by the door, her gentle smile brightening the dim hallway.

"Goodbye, Arwin!" she called out, her voice warm and cheerful. "Don't stay out too late!"

"Goodbye, Mrs. Carter!" he replied, his tone buoyed by the excitement still swirling in his mind. The possibilities of the day lingered with him, filling his thoughts as he stepped outside.

The moment he emerged onto the street, the cool evening air washed over him, a refreshing contrast to the warmth of the basement. The sky was painted in hues of orange and purple, the last remnants of daylight slipping away, and the streetlights flickered to life one by one.

He was completely amazed by the concept Dr. James had shared. The idea that light, which often felt so ordinary, could hold the power to reveal the past and glimpse the future left him in a state of wonder. He found himself pondering how something invisible could carry such significance.

Lost in his thoughts, Arwin didn't even notice the world around him fading into the background. The concepts Dr. James had introduced swirled through his mind, making the journey home feel like a dream. The evening air was cool against his skin, but he was oblivious to the chill, wrapped up in his fascination with the invisible light that could unveil the past and the future.

The streets blurred into a haze of colors as he wandered, the sounds of the evening muffled by the intensity of his thoughts.It wasn't until he stood at his front door, that he snapped back to reality. He blinked, surprised to find himself home, as if he had traveled not just through space but through time itself.

The familiar sight of the front door bringing a mix of comfort and apprehension. As he rang the bell, a knot of anxiety formed in his stomach. He feared his parents would scold him for losing track of time. A moment later, the door swung open, revealing his father, who wore a welcoming smile.

"So, you're back, Arwin," his father said, his tone

surprisingly gentle. There was a warmth in his eyes that eased Arwin's tension, even if he still braced himself for the inevitable conversation.

"Yeah, Dad," Arwin replied, stepping inside, his mind racing with worries about his parents' reactions.

Just then, his mother appeared from the kitchen, her expression shifting from relief to concern as she saw him.

"You should have told us where you were!" she exclaimed, her voice laced with worry. "You know how upset we were waiting for you."

Arwin glanced at his mother, his earlier excitement fading under her gaze. "I'm sorry, Mom. I got carried away ... I was talking with James about some ideas, and I lost track of the time."

His mother sighed, her expression softening but still holding an edge of disappointment. "I understand, but you need to communicate with us. We care about you, and it's important for us to know you're safe."

"I know," he said, feeling a wave of guilt wash over him. "I didn't mean to worry you."

His father stepped forward, placing a reassuring hand on his shoulder. "It's okay, son. We're just glad you're home now. Next time, just give us a call, alright?"

Arwin took a deep breath, the weight of his father's gaze pressing down on him.

"Yes, Father, I will tell you everything. I promise I won't keep things from you like this again."

Arwin picked up his mother's phone, ready to call Kelvin and share the news about his meeting with Dr. James. However, just as he was about to dial, he paused. A thought crossed his mind: perhaps it would be better to tell Kelvin in person. He imagined the thrill of watching Kelvin's face light up as he revealed the incredible details, the anticipation of their conversation building as they spoke.

Feeling a rush of excitement at the idea, Arwin set his phone down, choosing to save the moment for when they could see each other. He knew that sharing this experience in person would deepen their friendship and make the revelation even more meaningful. With a sense of purpose, he looked forward to the school day, eager to share his adventure.

His mother looked at him curiously, her concern momentarily replaced by intrigue.

"So, how did your meeting with that great scientist go?

What were his reactions?" she asked, her eyes bright with interest.

Arwin's face lit up, his earlier worries fading as he recalled the conversation. "He had a different point of view," he said, a hint of enthusiasm creeping into his voice.

"Dr. James is brilliant! He makes physics feel like magic," Arvin exclaimed, his eyes shining. "He has this way of explaining things that makes everything so clear and fascinating. I liked his ideas so much!"

He leaned closer, lowering his voice as if sharing a grand secret. "And guess what? He has space suits! Actual space suits! With those, I could go to space! Can you imagine?

His words tumbled out in a rush, painting vivid pictures of what it would be like to wear a suit designed for the stars, to feel the thrill of weightlessness, and to gaze down at Earth from above.

"He told me about the mysteries of the universe and praised me for my ideas. It felt incredible." His mother raised an eyebrow, intrigued. "Praise? From him?"

"Yeah!" Arwin replied, a smile spreading across his face. "It was the first time I enjoyed talking like this, discussing concepts I've only dreamed about. He made everything feel possible, and I realized there's so much more to learn."

His mother smiled, her initial worry softening as she listened to the excitement in her son's voice.

"I'm glad to hear that, Arwin. It sounds like you had a truly inspiring experience."

"Absolutely" Arwin said, feeling a renewed sense of motivation swell within him.

"I can't wait to dive deeper into these ideas." The fear that had lingered in his chest began to dissipate as he shared his passion, transforming the moment into one of connection and understanding with his parents.

"You should have your dinner now; it's ready in the kitchen," his mother said, gently nudging him toward the dining area.

"Okay, Mom," he replied, a hint of reluctance in his voice as he made his way to the kitchen. He ate quickly, still buzzing with excitement from his earlier conversation. The food was comforting, but his mind was elsewhere, replaying every detail of his encounter with James.

After finishing, Arwin headed to his room, the familiar surroundings feeling both safe and suffocating with anticipation. He climbed into bed, the soft sheets enveloping him, yet his thoughts raced. As he lay there, staring at the ceiling, he couldn't shake the questions swirling in his mind.

Why does it seem like time was moving so fast when I

was talking with Dr. James?" he pondered aloud, almost as if seeking an answer from the silence of his room. The moments spent in deep discussion had felt exhilarating, each second stretched into eternity, yet now they seemed like fleeting fragments of a dream.

The next day, Arwin hurried through his morning routine. The moment he stepped outside, the crisp morning air filled him with energy, and he quickened his pace toward school. Each step felt electric as he imagined Kelvin's reaction, the way his friend's eyes would widen in disbelief and excitement when he heard the news.

He arrived at school, but as he scanned the classroom, he noticed that his friend Kelvin hadn't shown up for the second consecutive day. A wave of disappointment washed over him; he had been eager to share the thrilling revelations and hear his friend's thoughts.

Throughout the morning, the absence of his friend nagged at him, worry creeping in. Why hadn't he come to school? Was everything okay? Arwin couldn't shake the feeling that something might be wrong. He decided that after school, he would swing by his friend's house to check in on him.

As he sat lost in thought, his physics teacher, Mr. Caldwell, approached with a playful grin.

"Did your parents have anything to say when you got home ?" he asked, trying to stifle a chuckle.

Arwin felt a flash of irritation but kept his expression neutral. He didn't want to engage in another round of teasing; he was still processing the anxiety from the previous night's confrontation. "No, nothing important," he replied, his toneflat.

Mr. Caldwell's grin faltered slightly, sensing Arwin's lack of enthusiasm. "Alright, just checking," he said, moving on to other students.

Arwin sighed inwardly, grateful to be free of further banter but still distracted by concern for his friend. He focused on the lesson, but his thoughts keptdrifting back to his absent companion. The day dragged on, and he could hardly wait for the final bell to ring so he could investigate.

As the final bell rang, Arwin bolted from the school, anxiety propelling him forward as he raced toward Kelvin's house.

He arrived breathless and rang the doorbell, heart pounding in his chest. When the door opened, he was taken aback by the sight of Kelvin's mother.

Her eyes were red and puffy, as if she had been crying recently.

Arwin felt a pang of concern. "Oh no," he thought to himself, sensing that something was seriously wrong.

"Yes, what do you need, child?" she asked, her voice slow and heavy with emotion.

"I'm Kelvin's friend, ma'am," Arwin replied, trying to keep his voice steady. "He hasn't come to school for two days, so I wanted to check on him."

Kelvin's mother struggled to hold back her tears, wiping them with her arm as she took a deep breath. "Please, come in," she said, stepping aside to let him enter.

Arwin hesitated for a moment, concern flooding his mind. "Has something happened, ma'am?" he asked, worry etched across his face.

"Is he okay?" She shook her head slowly, her expression filled with sorrow. "He's not well," she admitted, her voice cracking. "He's been struggling with some things ... it's been hard for him."

Arwin's heart sank. He could see that Kelvin's absence was more than just a temporary illness; it was something deeper. "Can I see him?" Arwin asked softly, hoping to offer some comfort to his friend during this difficult time.

Kelvin's mother looked down, her face reflecting the weight of her words.

"He's not at home. He's been admitted to the hospital," she replied, her voice trembling.

"I just came home to get some clothes for him. I'm on my way to see him now. You can come with me if you want."

Arwin's heart raced at the news. "I'll go with you," he said, eager to support his friend. "But can you please lend me your phone? I need to inform my parents that I'll be late."

"Of course," she said, handing him the phone. Arwin quickly dialed his home number, his fingers shaking slightly.

When his mother answered, he spoke quickly, "Mom, it's me. I'm going to be late because I'm going to the hospital to see Kelvin. He's not well." His mother's voice softened, filled with concern. "Okay, sweetheart. Just be careful and keep us updated."

"I will," he assured her before hanging up.

"Let's go," Kelvin's mother said, her voice regaining some composure. "You can sit in the car while I grab the things we need." Arwin nodded, relief flooding him at the thought of being there for Kelvin. They walked outside together, and she led him to her car.

As they drove through the streets, the tension in the car was palpable. Arwin, unable to shake off the heaviness in his heart, turned to Kelvin's mother.

"What happened to him?" he asked, his voice laced with grief.

"He was totally fine just two days ago."

Her grip tightened on the steering wheel, and she glanced at him briefly, her eyes filled with worry.

She sniffled, wiping her eyes with the back of her hand, but more tears kept coming. Her breath hitched as she struggled to find the words.

"The doctors say he's suffering from Quantum Cellular Decay Syndrome (QCDS)," she replied, her tone heavy with concern.

"It's a mysterious disease that causes a person's cells to break down really fast. It affects how their body works and leads to serious health problems."

Arwin's heart sank. He felt a lump in his throat. "Break down? How?"

"They don't know," she admitted, her voice quivering. "It's not like anything they've ever studied. His cells aren't just dying—they're collapsing. Disappearing. His body can't keep up with it." She paused, the weight of her words hanging in the air.

Arwin felt a chill run down his spine at the mention of the name. "How could this happen?" he asked, sorrow swelling within him.

Kelvin's mother sighed deeply, her expression troubled as she navigated the road. "The cause of QCDS can be linked to things like exposure to strange space radiation or issues related to new technologies," she explained, her voice tinged with frustration.

"That's what makes the disease so baffling- scientists don't fully understand it yet" and she quickly covered her mouth to stifle a sob.

Arwin listened in shock, trying to comprehend the gravity of the situation. The words "space radiation" and "new technologies" felt like something out of a science fiction novel, but here they were, affecting his friend in the most real and devastating way.

"Will he be fine?" Arwin asked, his voice trembling with concern, unable to hide the worry etched across his face.

Kelvin's mother glanced at him, her expression a mix of hope and fear. "The doctors are working hard to find a way to cure this disease," she reassured him, though her voice wavered slightly.

"They say they will do everything they can to save him."

Arwin nodded, clinging to her words like a lifeline. "I hope they can figure it out," he murmured, wishing he could do more than just wait.

As they approached the hospital, the towering building loomed ahead, a stark reminder of the uncertainty they were facing. Arwin's heart raced, a swirl of emotions churning within him-fear, hope, and a desperate need to support his friend.

He took a deep breath, steeling himself for what lay ahead, determined to be a source of comfort for Kelvin during this difficult time.

As they entered the hospital, the sterile smell of antiseptic filled the air, and the stark white walls only amplified the weight of the moment.

Arwin felt his heart race as he scanned the waiting area, and his breath caught in his throat at the sight of his friend's relatives sitting in chairs, their faces drawn and weary.

Among them, Arwin spotted Kelvin's father, his head buried in his hands, sobs racking his body.

"Harry, why are you crying?" Kelvin's mother exclaimed, her voice rising with panic. She rushed to her husband's side, a wave of dread washing over her.

"Is everything okay? Tell me!"

Overwhelmed by the gravity of her husband's despair and desperate for answers, Kelvin's mother wiped her tears and took a shaky breath.

She felt the urgency of the situation pressing down on her as she stepped away from Harry, who remained visibly shaken.

"Dr. Lenox," she called out, her voice firm despite the trembling in her hands. "I need to know what's going on with my son. Please, tell me the truth."

Dr. Lenox turned to face her, and the weight of his expression told her that he understood her fear. "Mrs. Hargrove," he began gently, "I wish I had better news. Kelvin's condition is critical.

Quantum Cellular Decay Syndrome is progressing at an alarming rate, and we've never seen a case evolve this quickly." The starkness of his words pierced through the air, and Kelvin's mother felt her heart

drop. "What does that mean?" she fought to maintain her composure. "Is there any hope for him?"

Dr. Lenox sighed, his brow furrowing with concern.

"We're doing everything we can to stabilize him, but the reality is that the technology we currently have is limited. The body's cells are breaking down at the quantum level. It's almost as if the very essence of his being is unraveling."

She gripped Dr. Lenox's arm, pleading for any glimmer of hope.

Dr. Lenox looked down, his expression somber and filled with regret. "I'm afraid there is no known treatment that can reverse the effects of Quantum Cellular Decay Syndrome," he replied gently. "We are doing everything possible to keep him comfortable, but
the truth is ...

"He paused, struggling to find the right words. "The reality is that there may be no way to save him."

The impact of his words hit Sarah like a physical blow. She staggered backward, tears streaming down her cheeks, her heart shattering into a million pieces.

"No ... it can't be. There must be something!" she cried, her voice breaking.

Harry joined her side, his own grief reflected in his eyes. "Please, Doctor," he urged, desperation filling his voice.
"There has to be something we can do. We can't lose our son!"

Dr. Lenox took a deep breath, his eyes filled with compassion. "I wish I could offer you more than this," he said softly. "But right now, the best we can do is make him as comfortable as possible and support him through this process."

Arwin watched helplessly from a distance, his heart aching for Kelvin and his family. The weight of the situation was unbearable, and he felt a profound sense of loss creeping in, even though
Kelvin was still alive. The thought of his friend suffering, coupled with the despair surrounding him, made the hospital room feel cold and dark.

Arwin couldn't stop the tears from welling up. His body felt heavy, his legs weak, and without thinking, he slumped against the wall and slid down to the floor. His heart pounded in his chest, his breath coming in ragged, shallow gasps. The tears he'd been fighting so hard to hold back finally broke through, spilling over his cheeks.

VII

For the first time, Arwin felt an emptiness where his usual curiosity about space and the mysteries of the universe once thrived. His thoughts were consumed by Kelvin, the gravity of his friend's situation overshadowing everything else.

His heart still raced, but not from excitement—not from dreaming of space, like it usually did. For the first time in his life, the vastness of space, the stars, Mars, all of it felt meaningless.

He didn't care about space anymore. He didn't care about rockets, or planets, or the idea of being the first human to set foot on Mars. All of those dreams, those wild plans he and Kelvin had talked about for hours, felt distant—like they belonged to another lifetime. Right now, the only thing that mattered was Kelvin.

Tears filled his eyes as he thought about his friend lying in that hospital bed, silent, fragile, fighting some terrible disease that Arwin couldn't even understand. All he wanted—more than anything—was for Kelvin to be okay. To see him sitting next to him, laughing, talking about their crazy talks like they always had.

But that felt so far away now. The fear of losing Kelvin, of never hearing his voice again, clawed at Arwin's chest, tightening his throat until he could barely breathe.

He wiped his face with his sleeve, staring blankly at the floor. The dream of going to space had always been their thing—something they held onto when everything else felt uncertain. But now, it didn't matter. Nothing did, if Kelvin wasn't there to share it with him.

The stars that usually inspired him now felt distant and irrelevant.

As Arwin wiping his tears, a sudden thought struck him like a spark igniting a fire. Dr. James!,

someone who dared to explore the boundaries of science. While he might not be a medical doctor, Dr. James had a way of seeing connections others missed, a knack for looking at problems from angles that seemed impossible.

In that moment, Arwin felt a flicker of hope igniting within him. Perhaps Dr. James could help. Perhaps he could offer insights or theories that could lead to something—anything—that might help Kelvin. Even if he didn't have a medical degree, his understanding of complex systems and innovative thinking might just unlock the key to saving his friend.

Wiping his face with the back of his hand, Arwin pushed himself up from the floor. "Dr. James can help," he whispered, each word strengthening his resolve. The more he thought about it, the more certain he became. He needed to find Dr. James, to share everything he knew about Kelvin's condition and to plead for his help.

Arwin felt an insistent pull to find Dr. James, his mind racing with thoughts of Kelvin and the dire situation he was facing. He wanted to meet with James, convinced that he might hold the key to a solution, some way to combat the overwhelming despair that had taken hold of him and Kelvin's family.

"I need to talk to him," Arwin said quietly, determination rising within him.

As he turned to leave the hospital, a sense of urgency coursed through him. The sterile corridors felt suffocating, filled with the sounds of hushed conversations and the beeping of machines that reminded him of the fragility of life. Each step he took propelled him forward, toward the hope that Dr. James might provide.

Arwin stood in the hospital lobby, the gravity of the situation weighing heavily on him. How can I get to Dr. James's home now? he thought, frustration building inside him. His family was so consumed by grief, they were in no condition to drive him anywhere.

He felt a wave of helplessness wash over him. The urgency of wanting to reach Dr. James clawed at him, and yet he was stuck here, unable to take action. The walls of the hospital seemed to close in around him, and he longed for a way out.

Arwin stood at the entrance of the hospital, anxiety twisting in his stomach.

He wanted to ask someone for help, but fear held him back. What if they're not trustworthy? he thought, glancing around at the unfamiliar faces bustling through the lobby.

The thought of approaching a stranger felt daunting, especially when he had no idea who they were or what their intentions might be. Just then, he noticed a group of hospital staff members walking nearby, their uniforms a comforting sight. They exuded professionalism and purpose, which made him feel a bit safer. Maybe it's different with them, he thought. They work here; they're supposed to help people.

Taking a deep breath, Arwin approached them hesitantly.

"Excuse me," he called out, his voice wavering slightly.

One of the staff members turned to him, a friendly smile on her face. "How can I help you?" she asked, noticing the concern in his expression.

Arwin felt a surge of urgency as he approached the group of hospital staff members.

"Can you please drop me at this address? It's very important," he pleaded, feeling the weight of his situation pressing down on him.

"Where do you want to go?" she asked.

"Green Garden," he replied quickly, hope flickering in his chest. "I really need to get there."

The staff members exchanged glances before one of them nodded. "Okay, child, sit tight. We'll drop you off. We're going that way," she said with a reassuring smile. Arwin's heart lifted at their kindness. "Thank you so much!" he exclaimed, relief washing over him. He climbed into the vehicle, feeling a renewed sense of purpose as they set off.

As Arwin sat in the back seat, unease washed over him. What if Dr. James doesn't have a solution? The fear of losing Kelvin gnawed at him. Taking a deep breath, he reminded himself, I have to believe there's hope.

The girl who had spoken to him earlier turned to him.

"What's at Green Garden that's so important?" she asked, genuine curiosity in her tone.

Arwin hesitated for a moment, weighing his options. He felt a connection with her, a spark of kindness in her voice that made him want to share. "It's... it's where my friend is," he said quietly, his voice barely above a whisper. "He needs me, and I just can't sit around waiting anymore."

Her expression softened, and she nodded as if she understood the weight of his words. "I get it. Friends are important," she said. "We'll get you there as fast as we can."

With that, the vehicle started moving, and Arwin felt a mix of anxiety and gratitude swell within him. The kind-heartedness of the staff wrapped around him like a warm blanket, easing the tension that had gripped him since he learned about his friend. As they drove through the city, he stole glances at the girl, who focused intently on the road, her long hair catching the sunlight in a way that reminded him of hope.

"Thank you again for helping me," he said, feeling the urge to express his gratitude once more. "It means a lot."

She glanced at him and smiled again, her eyes sparkling with warmth. "No need to thank us. Just hang in there, okay? We'll make sure you get to your friend." Arwin nodded, his heart buoyed by her support.

Once they drove away, he took a deep breath and headed toward Dr. James's house, his heart pounding with anticipation and hope.

Arwin approached Dr. James's door, his heart racing with anticipation. He knocked gently, and moments later, Mrs. Carter opened the door, her expression warm and welcoming.

"Hello there! What a pleasant surprise!" she exclaimed, her voice filled with kindness. "What brings you by today?"

"Hi, Mrs. Carter. Is Dr. James home?" Arwin asked, his urgency evident.

"Oh, yes! He's in the basement right now, busy with some experiments," she replied, a hint of admiration in her tone.

"Would you like me to take you to him?" Arwin nodded, feeling relieved by her willingness to help.

"Come this way," she said, gesturing for him to follow.

Arwin felt a flicker of hope as he followed her, grateful for her kindness and eager to reach Dr. James to discuss Kelvin's situation. As they walked through the house, she continued, "He's been working hard on some fascinating projects, but I'm sure he'll be delighted to see you.

Her words lifted his spirits, and he appreciated her encouragement as they made their way down the stairs. The soft sounds of tinkering grew louder with each step.

"Here we are," Mrs. Carter said, pausing in front of the basement door. "I hope he can assist you with whatever you need."

"Thank you, Mrs. Carter," Arwin replied, his heart brimming with hope.

Arwin bolted into the basement, his heart racing. Dr. James was bent over a large chalkboard, immersed in a complex equation filled with physics symbols and diagrams.

"Dr. James!" Arwin shouted, his voice cutting through the concentration in the room. "I need your help!" Startled, Dr. James turned around, eyes wide with surprise. "Arwin! What's wrong?" He quickly wiped his hands on his lab coat, concern etching his features.

"It's Kelvin!" Arwin exclaimed, breathless. "He's really sick, and I thought you might have a solution!"

Arwin's urgency grew. "He's the friend i was talking about when we were near the science museum! The one who loves science just like you."

Recognition dawned on Dr. James's face. "Ah, yes! I remember now. What's happened to him?" he asked, stepping closer.

Arwin took a deep breath, trying to steady his racing heart before diving into the story. "Dr. James, it's really serious. Kelvin has been absent from school for two days. I went to visit him, and his mom told me he's in the hospital. They said he has something called Quantum Cellular Decay Syndrome."

Dr. James's expression shifted, concern deepening as he listened intently. "Quantum Cellular Decay Syndrome? That sounds severe. What did the doctors say?"

"They told his parents that it's a mysterious disease that makes a person's cells break down really fast," Arwin continued, his voice trembling. "They don't fully understand it, but it can be linked to strange space radiation or new technologies. Dr. Lenox said it's almost impossible to treat with the current technology."

"I know Dr. Lenox," James said, reaching for his phone. "We met at the Great Science Hall last year. I'll give him a call."

As he dialed the number, there was no sense of uncertainty. Dr. James Carter was no ordinary man-he was a giant in the field of physics, and anyone in the scientific community would recognize his name.

The call connected quickly, and the voice on the other end was crisp.

"Dr. Lenox speaking."

"Hello, Dr. Lenox. This is Dr. James Carter," James said with his usual calm, knowing full well that his name carried weight. There was an audible pause, followed by an almost eager response. "Dr. James Carter? The James Carter?"

Lenox's voice was now warmer, laced with excitement. "It's an honor to hear from you. Your lectures and research papers-they've changed the way we look at particle physics. I've been following your work for years."
James smiled, a hint of pride surfacing. "Thank you, Dr. Lenox. I'm glad to hear my work has made an impact."
I have something important to discuss with you," James said, easing into the reason for his call.

"Yes, Dr. James, how can I help you?" Dr. Lenox asked, his voice steady but filled with concern.

James wasted no time. "I'm calling because I need to know how Kelvin will be treated for QCDS. His best friend is someone I know, and he told me you're handling the case. Isn't there any way to cure him?" James's voice was tight, almost pleading.

Dr. Lenox sighed deeply, the weight of his answer already pressing on him. "No, Dr. James, I'm afraid there isn't another way. QCDS is-"

James cut him off, his mind racing. "But there has to be something. What about those experimental treatments? I've read about energy regeneration therapies. Can't you use those?"

Lenox shook his head, though James couldn't see him. His voice was firm but sympathetic. "Those therapies work on a macro level, dealing with physical cell rejuvenation, but QCDS is different. It affects the quantum structure of the cells themselves.

They don't just die; they collapse inward, disintegrating at the most fundamental level."

"I'm truly sorry, Dr. James," Lenox replied softly, understanding the pain behind his colleague's voice. "I wish there was more we could do."

James closed his eyes for a brief moment, taking in everything Dr. Lenox had said. The reality of the situation weighed heavily on him. He cleared his throat, forcing the words out. "Okay, thank you, Dr. Lenox," he said quietly before ending the call.

Turning around, he found Arwin standing there, his eyes filled with quiet hope, waiting for answers. James's heart sank as he walked over to him, his face clouded with sadness.

"Arwin ... " he began softly, his voice barely above a whisper. "I'm so sorry. There's nothing we can do." Arwin's face fell, the spark of hope quickly dimming. He stood in stunned silence, struggling to process the words. James placed a hand on his shoulder, his voice breaking slightly. "I wish there was something-anything- but the disease ... it's too advanced. It's beyond what medicine can fix right now."

Arwin's eyes filled with frustration and disbelief as he looked at James. "But you were saying just yesterday that everything is possible in this world," he said, his voice trembling with emotion. "And now you're telling me there's no way?"

James exhaled slowly, his own feelings of helplessness bubbling beneath the surface. He met Arwin's gaze, trying to steady his voice.

"Arwin, I still believe that. I do," he said softly, his tone firm yet filled with compassion. "Everything is possible, but with the technology we have right now, we're not there yet. We don't have the tools to fight this disease ... not today, not now."

James's voice softened even further, pleading with Arwin to understand. "Please, try to see it from where we stand. It's not that it's impossible forever. It's just ... impossible right now."

Arwin's anger slowly gave way to the painful reality, and his shoulders slumped. "So we're just supposed to accept that?"

James's heart broke at the sight, but he nodded. "For now ... yes. But I promise you, if there was anything I could do, I would."

"Okay, Dr. James," Arwin said, his voice barely holding steady. The grief was evident in his eyes, but it was more than just sadness-it was a deep sense of loss, as if something precious had been taken from him.

He swallowed hard, struggling to keep his composure. "I think ... I should go."

James moved forward, his hand reaching out, trying to offer comfort. "Arwin, wait, you don't have to leave. We can-"

But Arwin gently shook his head, stepping back. His eyes, once filled with excitement and curiosity about the universe, were now dulled with sorrow.

"No, I ... I need to go home," he murmured, his voice breaking slightly.

"Goodbye," he whispered, and before James could say another word, Arwin turned and walked away.

He had always imagined himself looking up at the stars, reaching out for them, believing that anything was possible. The grief in his chest tightened, making it hard to breathe. His dream wasn't just a goal-it was a part of who he was. And now, it felt like that part of him had been broken, lost in the vast, unforgiving silence of space.

Arwin pushed open the front door, feeling the weight of the world on his shoulders. His parents looked up from the living room, concern etched on their faces.

"How's Kelvin? Is everything okay?" his mother asked, worry in her voice.

Arwin swallowed hard, his heart heavy."Kelvin's really sick," he said, unable to meet their eyes. "He has QCDS, and ... there's nothing they can do."

His mother gasped, covering her mouth in shock, while his father stepped forward, placing a hand on Arwin's shoulder.

"What do you mean?"

"They said it's too advanced," Arwin whispered, his voice shaking. "He's my best friend, and ... and there's nothing we can do."

His mother pulled him into a tight embrace, tears in her eyes.

As Arwin stood in her arms, the grief he had been holding back surged forth. The dreams he had once shared with Kelvin felt shattered, like stars extinguished in the night sky.

Arwin trudged up the stairs, his heart heavy with grief. He closed the door to his room, skipping dinner, feeling it would be pointless. Instead, he flopped onto his bed, avoiding the night sky that once inspired him; tonight, it felt cold and distant. Arwin lay wide awake in his bed, the shadows of his room pressing in on him. Each tick of the clock seemed to mock his anxiety, and his mind was a whirlwind of worry. What was Kelvin's condition? Images of their shared adventures filled his thoughts. Those memories felt like lifelines amidst the uncertainty.

After a few hours of tossing and turning, Arwin finally drifted off into a restless sleep.

That's when the dream began-strange, vivid, unlike any he had ever experienced before. In the dream, someone had entered Dr. James's house and made their way to the storeroom. In the middle of the room, a man in a black night suit was speaking with someone, though the details of the person he was talking to were unclear. The unknown person asked sharply,
"What are you doing here?"

The man in black responded, almost pleading, "I'm here to do something very important."

The air in the dream felt heavy with tension, and the conversation seemed important, though Arwin couldn't fully grasp it. Then the man in black added, "Antimatter is the solution to save him." Then he shouted "yes i am coming".

But before he could understand what was happening, the scene began to blur, and everything faded.

Arwin jolted awake, drenched in sweat and breathing

heavily. Though it was just a dream, it left him feeling shaken and filled with fear.

"What was that dream?" Arwin wondered, still feeling unsettled. The image of the man in the black lingered in his mind. Why did he say that only antimatter could help him?

Who was "him"? Was it Kelvin? He shook his head, trying to dismiss the thoughts. It was just a dream, he told himself. It's not real. But the man's words echoed in his mind, leaving him with a sense of unease.

As he lay back down, the images began to fade, Suddenly, Dr. James's words came back to him: "Dreams are a way of communication."

Arwin's heart raced. Could this dream be trying to tell him something important? Was it a warning about Kelvin? He took a deep breath, feeling the weight of the dream settle over him again.

"I should go check the storeroom of Dr. James's house," Arwin thought, his mind racing with possibilities. Why did that man go there? What if he was an alien from a higher dimension, trying to help them? But then he wondered, Why would they want to help us?

As more questions flooded his mind, he found himself pondering the meaning of antimatter. What exactly is antimatter? But could it really be a solution to save someone like Kelvin?

"What time is it?" Arwin asked himself, glancing at the clock. It was 5 a.m. I should go to Dr. James's house.

He quietly made his way downstairs, careful. The main door was locked, so he grabbed the key from its usual spot. After unlocking the door, he turned back to his parents, who were still asleep.

With a determined heart, he gently shook them awake. "Mom, Dad, I need to go to Dr. James's house. I have to check the storeroom. It's important."

His parents blinked at him in confusion, their expressions shifting to concern.

"Arwin, it's early," his mother replied, her voice laced with worry. "What's this about?"

"I believe I might be able to help Kelvin," he explained earnestly. "If I can just find something there, it could make a difference. Please, I don't have much time. Even a small act from me might save his life!"

His parents exchanged skeptical glances, unsure if they should take him seriously. To them, it sounded like a childish idea, fueled by desperation. However, considering the recent events and how much Arwin had been affected by Kelvin's illness, they hesitated to outright deny him.

"Alright," his father finally said, his voice firm but understanding. "You can go, but be careful, and come back soon." Relieved, Arwin nodded, gratitude swelling within him. With their permission granted, he slipped out the door and began his journey to Dr. James's house, determination guiding his steps.

Arwin sprinted as fast as his legs could carry him, urgency propelling him forward. The early morning air whipped against his face, but he paid no mind to the chill; all he could focus on was reaching Dr. James's house. Finally, after what felt like an endless run, he arrived, panting and exhausted, at the doorstep.

Without hesitating, he banged on the door, his fists connecting with the wood in a frantic rhythm.

"Dr. James! Dr. James!" he yelled, desperation lacing his voice.

After several moments of relentless knocking, the door creaked open, revealing Dr. James, who stood there in his nightwear, looking groggy and slightly disheveled.

"Arwin? What happened? Is everything alright?" he asked, concern flickering across his face.

Taking a deep breath to steady himself, Arwin replied, "I had a dream, Dr. James. It was strange. There was a man in a black night suit who said something about antimatter. I need to know what it is and how it could help Kelvin."

Dr. James dismissed Arwin's urgency as a byproduct of the emotional strain he was under due to Kelvin's illness.

"Arwin, it's probably just the effects of everything that's happened," he said lightly, trying to calm the boy's apparent distress. "Dreams can be strange, especially in tough times like these." However, Arwin was not ready to let it go. His determination surged within him.

"Can I please go into your storeroom?" he asked, his voice steady despite the anxiety fluttering in his chest.

Dr. James paused, taken aback by the request.

"The storeroom?" he replied, a hint of confusion in his tone. "It's quite messy in there. We don't even go in there anymore. What do you think you might find?"

Arwin's heart raced at the thought of uncovering something significant. " I need to see if there's anything that could help Kelvin. Please, Dr. James. I feel like it might be important." His plea was earnest, fueled by a flicker of hope sparked by his dream.

"Okay, come inside," Dr. James said, stepping aside to let Arwin enter. As they made their way toward the storeroom, Arwin's excitement bubbled over.

"Dr. James, I've been in the basement to meet you before, but I can still show you where the storeroom is!" he exclaimed, his voice filled with enthusiasm. "I've seen all this in my dream. You were right-dreams really do have a connection to real life!"

As they navigated through the dimly lit corridor, Arwin confidently pointed to one of the doors. "This is the storeroom!" he declared.

Dr. James halted abruptly, a look of astonishment crossing his face. "How do you know this? You've never set foot here before," he queried, a mixture of surprise and intrigue evident in his tone.

In that moment, it dawned on them that they had neglected to bring the keys.
Dr. James turned to Arwin, a note of urgency creeping into his voice. "Stay here, please. I need to retrieve the keys."
But an unsettling sensation washed over Arwin at the thought of being left alone in the familiar surroundings.

"No, I want to come with you," he replied, his voice trembling slightly. "I'm feeling a bit scared being here by myself."

Mrs. James led Arwin down the familiar hallway, the warm light spilling in from the windows illuminating the photographs that adorned the walls. Each frame told a story, capturing joyful moments of Dr. James's parents.

Arwin stared at the photo frames on the wall, his brow furrowing in confusion. They were Dr. James's parents—pictures taken long before. But something was off.

"Dr James," Arwin said slowly, pointing to the frames. "Your parents... they're in every frame." , couldn't help but asked, "Why are they alone in every photo? Where are you?"

At the question, James's gaze dropped, the light in his eyes dimming. A silence settled between them, thick and uncomfortable. He finally murmured, "I don't know." His voice was barely above a whisper, and Arwin could sense the weight of unspoken words hanging in the air.

James remained quiet, his expression inscrutable. It was clear there was a story there, but whether he was unwilling or unable to share it. Then they entered the room. James walked straight to the desk, his expression focused. He opened the drawer and rummaged through the clutter, finally pulling out a set of keys.

After retrieving the keys, they returned to the storeroom, a mix of excitement and apprehension swirling in the air.

James took a deep breath and turned the key in the lock, slowly pulling the door open. Instead of the usual dust and dirt that cluttered the storeroom, Arwin and Dr. James saw something else entirely, what lay before them was astonishing. An expanse of sand stretched endlessly, glimmering in shades of burnt orange, and soft gold. Strange rock formations jutted from the ground, their surfaces reflecting the light in brilliant hues. The sky overhead was a surreal tapestry of deep indigo and swirling clouds tinged with pink and purple.

James fell to the ground, Arwin's instincts kicked in. He hurriedly closed the door, aware that no one could survive in the strange environment beyond-its atmosphere was far too different from Earth's.

"Dr. James! Are you okay?" Arwin called out, kneeling beside his mentor, his pulse quickening with worry. The room felt heavy with uncertainty. Just then, Mrs. Carter rushed in, drawn by the shouting. "What happened?

James?" she exclaimed, her voice filled with alarm as she joined Arwin at his side.

"What happened to James?" Mrs. Carter asked sharply, her voice filled with concern as she rushed to his side. Her gaze flicked between Arwin and James, desperately trying to understand what had occurred.

"He was fine before you came! What did you do to him?" Arwin's heart raced, and he felt tears prickling at the corners of his eyes. "I-I don't know!" he stuttered, his voice barely above a whisper.

"We opened the door, and then he just fell! It was like he couldn't handle what he saw!"

Mrs. Carter quickly soaked a cloth with water, her hands trembling as she pressed it to James's forehead.

"James, please wake up!" she urged, her voice breaking with worry.

After a tense moment, James's eyelids fluttered open, revealing a look of confusion and disorientation. He blinked a few times, taking in the concerned faces hovering above him.

"What ... happened?" he croaked, his voice raspy.

"You passed out!" Arwin exclaimed, leaning closer. "You opened the door, and then you just collapsed!"

James's eyes widened as the memories flooded back to him, and a new understanding settled in.

"Yes, Arwin," he said, his voice steady but charged with intensity. "My studies were right- dreams do have a connection with reality. The dream you saw is the key to saving Kelvin. We need to explore it further."

Arwin, still shaken but encouraged by James's belief, nodded. "You really think it could help him?"

"Absolutely," James replied, leaning forward, urgency in his tone. "Tell me everything, Arwin. What did you see in your dream? Every detail matters." With a deep breath, Arwin began to recount the vision that had haunted him.

Arwin took a deep breath, recalling the vivid images that had played out in his mind. "I saw a man in a black night suit. He entered your storeroom and was talking to someone I couldn't see. The man in black said he was there for something important and mentioned that only antimatter could save. Arwin's brow furrowed as he recalled more details. "The man in black said he is coming to someone who was standing outside. But I couldn't see who it was."

James leaned in closer, his curiosity piqued. "Can't you recognize the voice? Do you remember anything about it?" Arwin shook his head, frustration evident in his expression. "No, it was different-completely unfamiliar.

"What is happening?" Mrs. Carter asked, her voice laced with concern.

"Arwin had a dream," James replied, still gathering his thoughts. "In it, the man in black mentioned that antimatter might be the key to saving Kelvin."

"Antimatter? How can that possibly save Kelvin?" Arwin pressed, his brow furrowing in confusion.

James sighed, rubbing his temples. "I'm not entirely sure. Antimatter is a complex topic-It interacts with regular matter in ways that can release a massive amount of energy. But how that could help with Kelvin's specific condition ...

I need to speak with Dr. Lenox. He's the one who understands these advanced concepts better than I do."

James took his phone from his pocket and scrolled through his contacts until he found Dr. Lenox's number. With a firm resolve, he tapped the screen and initiated the call, feeling a mix of hope and anxiety as he waited for the connection.

"Good morning, Dr. Lenox, sorry to disturb you so early," James said, his voice filled with urgency.

"You can call me anytime, Dr. James," came the calm reply from the other end. "Thank you," James said, taking a breath. "I need to ask you something important. How could antimatter possibly be the key to saving Kelvin?"

There was a pause on the line, as Dr. Lenox processed the question.

Dr. Lenox responded, his voice serious, "Dr James, when antimatter comes into contact with regular matter, they annihilate each other and release an immense amount of energy-light and heat. This process is incredibly powerful. We theorize that this energy could be harnessed to heal cells breaking down due to QCDS. If the energy from antimatter could be controlled, directed carefully, it could theoretically repair the damaged cells at the quantum level."

James listened intently as Lenox continued, "But, that's just it. It's all theory. We don't even know for sure if antimatter exists in any significant amount within our reach. If it does, it could be light years away. Right now, we have no real idea where it might be, how to harvest it, or how to control it if we did. It's a possibility that exists purely in theory."

"Oh, but if we had antimatter, would you be able to cure Kelvin?" James asked, desperation clear in his voice.

Dr. Lenox sighed heavily. "James, I respect you deeply, but

you need to understand-it's impossible. Antimatter simply doesn't exist on Earth. It's not something we can just find or create easily."

"But if we had it?" James pressed. "If we had it," Lenox said, his tone softening, "we would try anything. If we could somehow control it, there's a chance we could use its energy to repair the damage QCDS is doing to Kelvin's cells. But ... it's a dream. Right now, it's beyond our reach."

James took a deep breath and asked Dr. Lenox one final question, "How much time does Kelvin have left?"

"Only three to four days," Lenox replied, his voice tinged with concern.

"Thank you," James said, feeling the weight of the news.

With that, James ended the call, a sense of urgency pushing him forward. He turned to Mrs. Carter and Arwin, eager to relay the conversation. "I spoke with Dr. Lenox," he said, his tone infused with a mix of determination and optimism. "Kelvin still has three to four days. We can do something about this."

A spark of hope ignited in Arwin's eyes. "What's the plan?"

James continued, "We must approach this with confidence. If they've given us the portal, they'll surely provide guidance as well." He paused, allowing the weight of their mission to settle in.

"Let me go find the antimatter," he declared, determination etched on his face.

"I will return soon, I'll find a way to save Kelvin."

“I will also go with you. I won't let you go alone,” Arwin said firmly, meeting James's gaze with a steady resolve. The warmth of his words wrapped around James like a reassuring blanket, easing the tightness in his chest.

Arwin, determination shining in his eyes, replied, "The stars were once my destination, but now they are my responsibility. Kelvin is my friend, and they have communicated with me. It's important for me to go."

James hesitated, knowing the risks involved in the journey ahead. "Arwin, I appreciate your courage, but it could be very dangerous. I can't risk your life."

But After a long pause, James considered Arwin's words. The connection they shared with the higher-dimensional beings made this quest feel like more than just a mission; it was a shared purpose.

Finally, with a heavy sigh, he relented. "Alright, you can come with me, but you must promise to follow my instructions carefully. This isn't a game."

"Thank you, Dr. James! I promise I'll be careful!" Arwin exclaimed, a spark of hope igniting within him.

Mrs. Carter urged them, "You both need to leave now; time is not on your side." With a shared sense of urgency, they made their way to the basement, heading toward the astronaut suits.

As James prepared the gear, a wave of pride washed over him. This was the culmination of his hard work-the astronaut suits were finally being put to good use.

Turning to Arwin, he said firmly, "You must keep your suit on at all times in space, no matter the circumstances. Do you understand?"

"Absolutely, Dr. James. I won't take it off," Arwin replied, determination in his voice.

With that, they finished suiting up, ready to face the unknown that awaited them.

James looked at Mrs. Carter with a serious expression. "Emily, please let Arwin's parents know that he'll be late coming home today, or tomorrow. He's with me for a science exhibition." Emily's brow furrowed with worry. "James, we could be putting Arwin in serious danger."

With unwavering determination, James responded, "I won't let anything happen to him. If it comes down to it, I would sacrifice my own life to save him."

His words deeply touched Arwin, filling him with a mix of gratitude and determination. Then they dressed in their astronaut suits, Arwin glanced down, surprised. "I always heard these suits were heavy. But this ... it's almost like wearing nothing."

James, in a rush and full of tension, blurted, "These aren't your typical astronaut suits. They're designed with cutting-edge technology for comfort and mobility."

As they approached the storeroom, the air felt tense. Standing in front of the door that held the portal to the unknown, they turned to Mrs. Carter for what could be their final goodbye.

Her eyes shimmered with unshed tears, the weight of their mission heavy on her heart. "Good luck," she whispered, her voice tight with emotion, knowing they were about to embark on a journey into the vast, infinite reaches of space.

IX

Emily wrapped her arms around them, drawing strength from the moment. Her heart raced with a mix of hope and apprehension as she whispered, "I hope for the best."

Dr. James, his voice steady but filled with concern, replied from inside his helmet, "Emily, you need to go out of the room now; it could be dangerous." The weight of his words sank in, and with a determined nod, Emily stepped out into the unknown.

James followed closely behind, his own excitement mingling with caution as he opened the door. The air felt charged with anticipation, and a sense of adventure coursed through him. Arwin stood at the threshold, his mind racing with thoughts of the night he had spent gazing at the stars. Each twinkling light had ignited his imagination, and now he was on the brink of stepping into that very cosmos he had always longed to explore.

"Are you ready, Arwin?" James asked, his voice crackling through the comms.

"Yes," Arwin replied, his voice steady, though his heart raced with a mixture of fear and exhilaration.

As they opened the door, they found themselves on a landscape of burnt orange sand, the ground shifting gently beneath their feet. The colors were vibrant, almost otherworldly, and the sky above glowed with a brilliant hue. To their astonishment, they felt an unusual lightness, as if the very laws of gravity had changed. Arwin could hardly believe it-he jumped, and to his delight, he soared high into the air, weightless and free.

"Arwin, you can still go back if you're scared,"

James offered, his tone reassuring yet firm. "No way! The universe can't scare me," Arwin replied with newfound confidence, his eyes sparkling with wonder. "Great!" James said, his enthusiasm infectious.

"Where are we?" Arwin asked, scanning the alien landscape with wide eyes, curiosity bubbling within him. "I don't know," James admitted, glancing around at the unfamiliar terrain. "Maybe thousands of light- years away. This planet isn't part of our solar system," he explained through his helmet, his voice filled with awe and uncertainty.

Arwin turned to Dr. James, concern etched on his face. "Dr. James, Kelvin will be okay, right?" he asked, his voice laced with anxiety.

"Yes, absolutely," James replied, his tone firm and reassuring. Yet, despite his confident words, Arwin could sense the lingering worry in James's eyes. The specter of Kelvin Syndrome hung over them, a shadow that made the adventure feel heavy despite the excitement of being on this new planet.

As they stood together, their attention was suddenly drawn to the sky. Arwin's jaw dropped in astonishment. Two suns blazed brightly above them, casting an unusual glow over the landscape. The suns shone brilliantly against the backdrop of a violet sky, bathing the burnt orange sand in shades of deep purple and gold.

"Wow," Arwin breathed, his awe palpable. He had never seen anything like it; the dual suns created an otherworldly light that made the landscape shimmer as if it were alive. The sight was mesmerizing, and for a moment, the worries about Kelvin and their mission faded away, replaced by pure wonder.

Dr. James gazed upward as well, his previous worries momentarily eclipsed by the breathtaking beauty of the scene. "It's incredible," he said softly, marveling at the celestial display." I wonder what other wonders this planet holds."

Arwin's excitement bubbled to the surface. "This is amazing! Imagine the stories we could tell to Kelvin," he said, his eyes sparkling with enthusiasm.

"Where do we get antimatter?" Arwin asked, his brow furrowed in concern. The thought of finding something so powerful weighed heavily on him.

"If the portal is opening on this planet, it means that antimatter could be here," Dr. James replied, scanning the horizon with intent determination.

"We need to find it." Arwin's eyes widened at the prospect. "But will we be able to bring it back with us? I mean, can we just pick it up with our hands?" James shook his head, his expression grave.

"No, Arwin. Antimatter is not something you can just pick up. It's incredibly volatile. Just one gram of antimatter contains around 180 trillion joules of energy." Arwin felt a shiver run through him. "That's... a lot of energy."

"Exactly," James continued, his tone serious. "To put it into perspective, the atomic bomb dropped on Hiroshima released about 63 trillion joules of energy. So, one gram of antimatter would unleash almost three times that amount. It's the most powerful substance known to man."

Arwin's heart sank at the implications. "So, it could destroy the world?" he asked, his voice almost a whisper. "Yes," James confirmed, his gaze unwavering. "We need to handle this with extreme caution. If we find it, we'll need specialized equipment to contain it safely. One mistake could lead to catastrophic consequences." A mixture of fear and determination filled Arwin. The idea of harnessing such immense power was daunting.

As Arwin and Dr. James walked alone on the unknown planet in their space suits, the weight of their mission pressed heavily on their minds. The vast landscape stretched endlessly before them, a tapestry of burnt orange sand and vibrant, alien flora, all under the watchful gaze of the two suns. They were searching for something powerful and elusive, yet neither of them knew exactly where to begin. A sense of determination drove them forward, but as they traversed the unfamiliar terrain, a question surfaced in Arwin's mind-one that had been overshadowed by the breathtaking beauty of the moment when they first arrived.

"Dr. James," he began, glancing up at the radiant dual suns illuminating the violet sky," why does this planet have two suns?"

James paused for a moment, considering the question. "That's an interesting observation." This is a binary star system," Dr. James explained, his eyes scanning the skies where the two suns glowed brightly.

"Binary star systems form when a dense region of a molecular cloud collapses under gravity. This collapse can fragment into two or more clumps, each forming a protostar. As these protostars develop, they interact gravitationally, establishing orbits around a common center of mass. Eventually, they become main sequence stars, completing the binary system." Arwin listened intently, fascinated by the complexity of the cosmos.

"So, are planets in binary star systems habitable?" he asked, his curiosity piqued.

James nodded, his tone thoughtful. "Yes, planets in binary star systems can be habitable, but several factors are crucial." He held up his fingers, preparing to list them. "First, the planet must have a stable orbit to remain in the habitable zone. This is the region around a star where conditions are just right for liquid water to exist."

"The distance between the stars matters significantly. If they are too close together, the gravitational forces can destabilize the orbits of any planets, making it difficult for them to maintain the right conditions for life." James continued, "The planet's composition is also vital, including its atmosphere and surface conditions. A planet with a suitable atmosphere can regulate temperature and protect against harmful radiation, while surface conditions like temperature, pressure, and the presence of water are essential for supporting life."

Arwin gazed up at the twin suns through the visor of his helmet, pondering the possibilities.

"So, if this planet has the right conditions, it could potentially support life?"

"Exactly," James confirmed.

"But we have to focus on our primary goal. The potential for habitability here is fascinating, but we need to stay on track. We're here to find antimatter and save Kelvin." With that reminder, Arwin felt a renewed sense of purpose. The wonders of the universe surrounded them, but their mission was clear.

As they ventured deeper into the alien terrain, James suddenly halted, a look of intrigue crossing his face. "Arwin, come here! You need to see this, Footprints!" He knelt down, brushing aside the fine, burnt orange sand to reveal a series of unusual markings on the ground. The footprints were significantly larger than any human's, their elongated shapes creating deep impressions that seemed to tell a story of their own.

Arwin crouched beside him, his heart racing with a mix of curiosity and anticipation. "These footprints... they're massive! Look at the size of them! They must belong to the beings we sensed earlier. Maybe they're here to help us!" His voice brimmed with hope, envisioning a friendly encounter that could turn the tide of their mission. But James furrowed his brow, skepticism clouding his expression.

"I don't think so," he replied, his tone measured and cautious. "If they truly wanted to assist us, they could have given us the antimatter directly, right? Why go through the trouble of bringing us here instead of just helping us outright?"

Arwin glanced down at the footprints again, a nagging doubt creeping into his mind. The trail led deeper into the alien landscape, hinting at the potential for discovery-or danger. "You might be right," he admitted slowly, the excitement of the moment giving way to caution. "But we need to follow them. We can't turn back now."

With a shared glance of determination, they stood up, ready to tread the uncertain path ahead, aware that each step could lead them closer to answers -or peril.

Arwin hesitated, his brow furrowed as he recalled the vivid images from his dream. "What I saw in my dream were humans," he confessed, a sense of unease creeping into his voice.

James frowned, shaking his head in disbelief.

"That can't be the reason for everything happening here," he replied, his tone firm. "They might have fabricated that story as a way to manipulate us. It's possible they created those visions to draw us here, leading us to think we can trust them."

Arwin's heart raced as he processed this idea. "So you're saying they're using our dreams as a tool to influence us? To shape our understanding of their intentions?"

"Exactly," James said, his eyes narrowing as he contemplated the implications. "By presenting themselves as familiar figures, they might be trying to establish a connection with us. "It's possible they created that narrative to guide us, to make us more receptive to their intentions. We have to be cautious; there's more at play here than we realize."

"But whatever they are, it seems like they're helping us," James began, his voice thoughtful yet cautious. "But we need to be very careful on this planet. It's not guaranteed that the ones helping us are actually from here. Just look around- this place is barren, is.

The aliens that live here don't seem advanced enough to have created a portal. If they had that kind of technology, this planet would look very different, more developed, more sophisticated."

He gestured toward the vast, empty landscape. The ground stretched endlessly, no structures, no technology- just endless sand and rock beneath the violet sky. Arwin looked around, taking in the desolate surroundings. "You're saying the ones who built the portal might not be the same aliens that live here?" he asked, trying to make sense of it all.

"Exactly," James replied. "There's no way this planet's inhabitants, if they're even still here, could manage something so advanced. If they were capable of creating that kind of technology, we'd see evidence of it. Cities, advanced machinery- something. But all we see is this emptiness. Whoever is helping us might not even be from this planet, and that means we can't trust anything at face value." Arwin nodded slowly, understanding the gravity of what James was saying. "So, we're caught in something bigger than we realized."

"Right," James agreed. "We need to stay alert. Just because we're being helped doesn't mean we're safe. We don't know the full picture yet, and that means we have to be ready for anything."

X

"We need to get closer to the portal," James urged, his tone growing more serious. "Staying out here, alone, in someone else's world is too dangerous. We don't know what's lurking around."

As he spoke, a sudden, sharp beeping sound echoed from their astronaut suits. The noise sliced through the eerie quiet of the barren landscape, causing both of them to stop dead in their tracks.

"Arwin!" James shouted, his voice laced with urgency. "That's the danger alert!" Arwin looked down at his suit, panic rising as the beeping continued to intensify.

"What does it mean?" he asked, already knowing the answer but needing to hear it confirmed.

"It's the alien detector," James explained, eyes scanning the horizon. "The beeping means there are aliens nearby. Our suits are picking up their presence."

The barren, empty land that had felt lifeless just moments ago now felt charged with hidden threat. Arwin's pulse quickened as his gaze darted across the landscape, searching for any sign of movement, but there was nothing.

The silence only added to the tension. "They're close," James said, his voice low but steady. "And we have no idea if they're friendly or hostile. We can't stay out in the open like this."

Arwin nodded, fear bubbling just beneath the surface, but he kept his focus.

"'We have to get out of here!' Arwin's voice shook with fear, his helmet barely muffling the panic as he urged Dr. James to run."

Without another word, they adjusted their gear and began making their way toward the portal, every step now heavy with the awareness that something, or someone, was watching them. The beeping from their suits persisted, a constant reminder that they weren't alone.

As they sprinted toward the portal, Arwin quickly realized that the lower gravity on this planet allowed him to run faster and leap higher than he ever could on Earth. But that exhilaration was short-lived. Behind them, he began to hear unsettling sounds-scratching, shuffling, and something almost like a low, guttural growl. Panic surged within him, and he risked a glance over his shoulder. What he saw made his heart race even faster. A group of creatures was in pursuit, their forms grotesque and unlike anything he had ever encountered. They had no discernible faces, just smooth, featureless surfaces where eyes and mouths should be.

"Dr James!" Arwin shouted, fear gripping his voice. "Look back! We're being chased!" Before James could respond, the creatures seemed to quicken their pace, closing the distance between them. Their elongated limbs propelled them forward with an eerie grace, and Arwin felt a chill run down his spine.

"Keep moving!" James yelled, determination in his voice. "Don't look back!" Arwin turned his gaze forward, focusing on the portal that shimmered in the distance. They needed to reach it before the creatures caught up to them, but the alien landscape was filled with obstacles, and every step felt like a race against time. The sounds of the creatures grew louder, echoing in the stillness, a reminder that danger was not just behind them but all around them.

Without a second thought, they all stepped through the door, their movements swift and precise. No sooner had they crossed the threshold than alien creatures appeared from the shadows, moving with alarming speed. They were tall and menacing, their glowing eyes locked on the them, their clawed hands reaching out, desperate to capture them. The creatures closed in, just a breath away, their outstretched fingers nearly brushing against Arwin and James.

sooner had they crossed the threshold than alien creatures appeared from the shadows, moving with alarming speed.

They were tall and menacing, their glowing eyes locked on the them, their clawed hands reaching out, desperate to capture them. The creatures closed in, just a breath away, their outstretched fingers nearly brushing against them. But then, as if in response to the danger, a sudden, invisible force surged around them. It flared to life, an unseen barrier of power, stopping the aliens in their tracks.

The creatures recoiled in frustration, their hisses cutting through the air as they tried to push forward but were repelled by the protective field. The barrier held strong, shimmering faintly for a moment longer before fading, leaving them unharmed.

Arwin glanced around, his confidence unwavering. They had been saved.

"Where are we?" Arwin asked, his voice trembling as he scanned the surroundings.

Darkness stretched out in every direction, filled with swirling gases that seemed to pulse with energy. The air was thick, heavy with a presence he couldn't fully grasp. His heart raced, and the confusion in his voice was clear.

"We should be at your home!" Arwin's frustration boiled over. "Kelvin is fighting for his life, and we're stuck here! What is happening? I don't understand!" His fists clenched, and tears brimmed in his eyes as helplessness washed over him.

Suddenly, the total darkness around them shifted, as if a film had begun to play. The once empty void started to stir, and in front of their eyes, the beginning of the universe unfolded, much like a scene in a movie. What had been an endless blackness moments ago now came to life, filled with bursts of light and energy, swirling and expanding in every direction.

Earlier, they had been standing on a solid, pitch-black floor-an eerie space where everything felt still and lifeless. But now, the ground beneath their feet had vanished entirely, replaced by the vast openness of space. They were floating, suspended in the middle of the universe's creation.

It was as if the universe itself had awakened, transforming the black room they had been in into a living, breathing cosmos.

Arwin and James stood in awe, watching as the early moments of existence came to life, enveloping them in its magnificent, chaotic beauty.

James looked around, his face pale, but his eyes had a distant, knowing look.

"Arwin," he said softly, the sadness in his voice unmistakable.

"We're in the past."
"The past?" Arwin wiped the tears from his face, his breath catching. "What do you mean?"

James sighed, his gaze drifting towards the strange, glowing light that swirled through the darkness like a cosmic storm.

"We're at the beginning, Arwin. We're witnessing the universe right after the Big Bang."
Arwin's eyes widened, taking in the scene around them.

The once incomprehensible darkness now seemed alive, filled with something ancient, yet strangely new. The air shimmered with an intense heat, though it felt oddly distant.

instant, it transformed. Suddenly, the vast expanse of the universe's beginning exploded into view, with bursts of light and energy swirling around them. They were no longer in the room-they were floating in the very heart of the Big Bang.

Arwin's eyes widened as he floated next to Dr. James, both of them suited up in their astronaut gear, gazing out into the infinite expanse of space. They were floating in the void, tethered to nothing but each other, witnessing the beginning of the universe itself.

"This is it," Arwin whispered, his voice filled with awe. "The start of everything."
Before them, an unimaginably bright, dense point of light erupted in silence. In a fraction of a second, the explosion expanded outward, faster than they could comprehend, sending waves of searing energy through the darkness. The light flickered and pulsed as the universe took its first breath.

"The Big Bang," Dr. James said, his voice steady but tinged with reverence. "This is how it all began."
Around them, the chaos unfolded- quarks, the smallest known particles, zipped around, colliding, combining, and breaking apart in a fiery dance. They moved too fast to follow, forming a hot, dense soup that filled every inch of space.

"Those...those are quarks!" James exclaimed. "They're forming protons and neutrons!"
"Why aren't we burned by all this energy?" Arwin asked, his voice filled with both wonder and fear.
James replied, "Because it's like a movie is playing out before us. We're witnessing this moment from a distance, as if we're observers in a grand cosmic theater."

As the seconds passed, the universe continued to expand. Arwin could feel the raw power of creation coursing through the air, making his skin tingle with energy.
"Do you see that?" James pointed at a swirling mass of energy. "Those are the first atoms forming!"
"Hydrogen and helium!" Arwin exclaimed, recognizing the building blocks of the universe. "This is the beginning of stars!"

Indeed, as they watched, clouds of gas began to clump together, drawn by gravity. Over millions of years, these clouds would ignite to form the first stars. They could hardly contain their excitement.
"Imagine what comes next!" Dr James said. "These stars will eventually explode, scattering heavier elements across the universe. That's how planets and life begin!"

"Everything we know is born from this moment," Arwin said, his mind racing. "From the dust of stars to the Earth beneath our feet!"

As the universe continued to expand, the darkness filled with glittering points of light. Galaxies began to form, spiraling and clustering in a dance of creation.

As Arwin and James continued to witness the awe-inspiring spectacle of the universe's birth, the initial chaos of the Big Bang began to settle into a more organized form. The swirling clouds of gas and dust coalesced, gradually taking shape as stars ignited in a blaze of brilliance. Each star became a beacon of light, illuminating the vast darkness of space.

"Look at those clusters," Arwin said, pointing toward a distant them of stars forming a beautiful spiral. "Those are galaxies coming together!"

"Yes!" James replied, glancing around nervously. "And among those stars, some will eventually form solar systems, just like ours."

Time flowed differently in this cosmic realm. Millions of years passed in mere moments for Arwin and James as they witnessed the birth of countless stars, their fiery cores fusing hydrogen into helium. Some of these stars grew massive, burning brightly for millions of years before eventually reaching the end of their life cycles.

"What happens when a star dies?" Arwin asked, unease creeping into his voice.

"Do you see that one?" James pointed to a colossal star glowing intensely.

"It's about to go supernova!" "What's a supernova?" Arwin inquired, his eyes wide with apprehension.

"It's when a massive star exhausts its fuel and explodes in a spectacular burst of energy," James explained. "The explosion scatters heavy elements- carbon, oxygen, iron- across the cosmos.

Those elements are crucial for forming new planets and eventually life!" Arwin swallowed hard as he watched the star swell and then erupt in a cataclysmic display of light and color.

"So... it just blows up? That seems dangerous."

"Yes," James admitted, his voice low. "But it's also necessary. After the explosion, the remnants will form new clouds of gas and dust, enriching the universe with the elements needed for life."

"Are we going to see the formation of new planets?" Arwin asked, his voice trembling slightly.

The scene shifted again, and Arwin and James found themselves in a swirling disk of gas and dust orbiting a young, bright star-our Sun.

Over time, the particles collided and fused, gradually forming larger and larger bodies.

"Look at that!" Arwin pointed at a small, molten sphere that was slowly cooling.

"That's our early Earth!" "Yes!" James replied, glancing around as if expecting danger.

"As it cooled, the surface began to solidify, forming a crust. But it's still inhospitable-lots of volcanic activity and meteor impacts."

"Will it always be like this?" Arwin asked, his heart racing at the sight of the fiery landscape.

"No, it will change," James assured him. "Time will transform this planet. Water vapor will accumulate, and rain will fill the basins, creating the first oceans."

"As it cooled, the surface began to solidify, forming a crust. But it's still inhospitable-lots of volcanic activity and meteor impacts."

The landscape was harsh and chaotic, with fiery lava flows and violent eruptions. The atmosphere was thick with gases, making it unlivable for any known life forms. As they continued to observe, they saw the accumulation of water vapor in the atmosphere. Over time, rain fell and filled the basins, creating the first oceans. The blue planet emerged, vibrant and full of potential.

"Isn't it amazing?" Arwin said, gazing at the swirling blue and green of the young Earth. As they continued to watch, simple life forms began to emerge-microscopic organisms that thrived in the warm, shallow oceans. These tiny organisms were the ancestors of everything that would follow.

The planet transformed over millions of years. Continents drifted apart and collided, creating mountains and valleys. Life diversified, evolving from the smallest microbes to massive dinosaurs. Each new phase of evolution unfolded like a chapter in an epic tale. Time continued its relentless march forward, and the first plants began to emerge on land, followed by insects and larger animals. The ecosystem began to flourish, setting the stage for the rise of complex life forms. The scene shifted once more, revealing the emergence of early humans. Tribes roamed the land, discovering fire, creating tools, and forming communities. They began to understand their environment, learning to survive and thrive.

As the stars twinkled above them and the Earth continued to flourish with life, Arwin and James realized that their adventure had only just begun. The cosmos was vast, and the mysteries of the universe awaited them.

Together, they were ready to explore the wonders of existence, armed with the knowledge of where they had come from and the infinite possibilities that lay ahead.

As Arwin and James continued to observe the unfolding story of life on Earth, the scene shifted again. They found themselves in a lush, prehistoric landscape filled with vibrant plants and the sounds of various creatures. Massive dinosaurs roamed the land, while colorful insects flitted among the foliage.

However, their attention was drawn to a smaller them of creatures huddled together in a clearing.

"Look over there," James pointed, directing Arwin's gaze to a gathering of early hominids.

They were upright, with hair covering their bodies, but their faces bore a resemblance to both humans and their primate ancestors.

"These are the earliest ancestors of modern humans."

The hominids were using simple tools made of stone to gather food and build shelters. They communicated with each other using a rudimentary form of language, a series of grunts and gestures that conveyed basic emotions and needs.

"Are they evolving?" Arwin asked, watching intently as one of the hominids skillfully crafted a tool.

"Yes," James replied, observing the them. "

Over time, these early hominids will develop more advanced tools, language, and social structures. This is just the beginning of their journey."

As they watched, the hominids began to engage in cooperative hunting and gathering. They worked together to bring down larger animals, showcasing a growing sense of community. Fire flickered in the distance, illuminating their faces as they gathered around it for warmth and protection.

"Fire... that's a huge leap," Arwin noted, realizing its significance.

"It must change everything for them."

"Exactly," James said. "With fire, they can cook food, ward off predators, and stay warm during the night. It marks a crucial turning point in their development."

Days turned into weeks as Arwin and James witnessed the gradual evolution of these early hominids. They saw the gradual development of more sophisticated tools, the beginnings of art through cave paintings, and the establishment of social hierarchies. The once-simple thems transformed into complex societies, driven by shared knowledge and cooperation.

"Look at how they interact," Arwin observed, noticing a young hominid comforting an injured companion. "They're starting to show empathy."

"Yes," James acknowledged.

"Emotional connections are vital for survival. They'll form bonds that strengthen their communities, leading to the rise of family units and social structures." The scene continued to evolve, showcasing the emergence of language. The hominids began to communicate more effectively now.

The scene continued to evolve, showcasing the emergence of language.

The hominids began to communicate more effectively, developing a richer vocabulary that allowed them to share stories, express emotions, and pass on knowledge from one generation to the next.

"This is incredible," Arwin said, captivated by the growth of human culture.

"It's like they're discovering what it means to be human." As the years turned into centuries, Arwin and James saw the transformation of these early hominids into fully-fledged humans. They developed agriculture, learning to cultivate crops and domesticate animals, which allowed them to settle in one place and form more permanent communities.

"Now they're building civilizations," James remarked, watching as structures began to take shape in the distance, marking the dawn of human innovation and creativity. The growth of these civilizations led to advancements in art, science, and technology. Arwin and James marveled at the development of writing, architecture, and the establishment of trade routes that connected different cultures.

"From simple tool users to builders of great cities," Arwin said, reflecting on the journey.

"It's astonishing how far they've come." As they continued to witness the rise and fall of various cultures, the complexity of human life unfolded before them. The emergence of philosophy, religion, and the quest for knowledge shaped the human experience.

As they continued to witness the rise and fall of various cultures, the complexity of human life unfolded before them. The emergence of philosophy, religion, and the quest for knowledge shaped the human experience. The stars twinkled overhead, and Arwin felt a sense of connection to this remarkable journey.

"It all started from that moment of the Big Bang," he said softly.

"And look where we are now."

"Yes," James replied, a sense of wonder in his voice.

"The universe has a way of guiding life toward complexity and connection. We are part of this incredible story, and it all traces back to those first moments of creation." Together, they stood in awe of the intricate tapestry of life that had emerged, realizing that humanity's journey was just one chapter in the vast narrative of the cosmos.

As Arwin and James continued to navigate the ethereal expanse of the universe, the scene around them shifted abruptly.

They found themselves inside a brightly lit hospital room, the soft beeping of machines and the faint murmur of voices creating a surreal backdrop. In the center of the room, a doctor cradled a tiny infant, his features barely discernible as he swaddled the newborn in a soft blanket.

"It's a boy!" the doctor announced, his voice filled with joy. Next to him, a nurse carefully lifted a second infant, revealing James's twin sister. "And here's your daughter!" she said, placing her in their mother's arms, where the warmth of familial love filled the room. James felt a jolt of surprise as he observed this intimate moment.

"Wait... I have a sister?" he whispered, bewildered.

James watched as his parents beamed with pride and joy, their faces glowing with happiness as they held their newborns.

His mother cradled both children lovingly, whispering sweet words of affection, while his father stood beside her, tears of joy glistening in his eyes. However, the joyous scene began to darken, shifting rapidly as time flowed forward. The happy chatter faded, replaced by the urgent sounds of medical staff rushing in.

"What's happening?" James asked, his heart racing. "Why are we seeing this?"

The atmosphere became heavy as James watched helplessly. His mother, now pale and frail, lay in the bed, while his father looked frantic and desperate, calling for help. The joy had vanished, replaced by panic and confusion.

Suddenly, flames began to consume the walls, creeping closer to the room where his family lay. Medical staff scrambled to evacuate patients, the air thick with panic. His mother, too weak to move, clutched James and his sister tightly, while his father desperately tried to get help.

As the vision of the hospital continued to play out before them, James could suddenly hear voices cutting through the thick smoke and chaos. His mother's voice-soft but urgent-echoed in the room, as she cradled both him and his twin sister in her arms. The desperation in her voice sent a chill down his spine.

"You go out of the room fast," his mother said, her voice trembling but firm. She looked up at his father, her eyes filled with fear and love, pleading for him to leave and save himself. But James's father shook his head, tears streaming down his face.

"I won't let you die here," he replied, his voice cracking with emotion. His eyes were filled with the weight of the impossible choice before him, torn between saving his children and staying with his wife in their final moments. They locked eyes, both of them knowing what was coming but unable to abandon each other. The smoke thickened, and the heat from the fire pressed in on them, but their love and determination held firm.

Just then, the door burst open, and a nurse, coughing and shielding her face from the smoke, rushed into the room. She was panicked but focused, her eyes darting between the burning walls and the parents holding the newborns

. "Give me the boy and girl!" the nurse shouted over the sound of the roaring flames.

"I can save them! Please!" James's mother, tears streaming down her face, hesitated, her grip tightening on her children. But she knew what she had to do. Slowly, painfully, she handed her son and daughter to the nurse, her hands shaking as she let them go. "Take them," she whispered, her voice barely audible through her sobs. "Please... save them." The nurse took both babies in her arms.

As James and Arwin floated in space, watching the tragic scene unfold, the nurse rushed toward the door with both newborns in her arms. But then, in the chaos, something terrible happened. As she moved through the smoke-filled corridor, her foot slipped on the wet hospital floor. She stumbled, barely keeping her balance, and in that moment of confusion, she lost her grip. She quickly regained her footing, but in her haste, she hadn't realized something crucial-she was only holding one baby. James's heart pounded in his chest as he watched the nurse rush through the exit, cradling only him.

James's father glanced at his wife one last time, his face etched with sorrow. "I'll stay with you," he said quietly, his voice breaking. He reached out, taking her hand as the flames closed in James, now a grown man, stood there helplessly, watching the memory unfold. He could hear the cries of his parents and see the desperate look on his father's face as he tried to save them. But it was too late. The flames consumed the room. The vision blurred, the smoke and fire consuming everything in its path, and then it all faded to black, leaving James and Arwin once again floating in the vast emptiness of space.

James's heart ached as the weight of the memory settled over him. Tears streamed down his face, his mind racing with questions, with the overwhelming grief of knowing how his family had been lost to him.

The beauty of the cosmos was breathtaking, yet it felt almost surreal given the emotional weight that hung in the air. James's heart raced as tears welled in his eyes, the recent revelations swirling in his mind like the nebulae around them. "Why is this great universe showing me my history?" he asked, his voice trembling with a mix of sorrow and sobbing.

Arwin, too, was shaken by the vision. He placed a hand on James's shoulder, his voice soft but steady. " Dr James, I'm so sorry. This... it's unimaginable. But it wasn't your fault, and it wasn't even the nurse's fault. It was a moment of chaos -a terrible accident." James clenched his fists, his body trembling with grief and anger. "I never knew," he said through gritted teeth. "I never knew any of this. Why didn't anyone tell me?

The scene faded to black, leaving only the echoes of James's cries, the realization of a family lost too soon settling heavily in his heart.

As the vision continued to unfold, James and Arwin found themselves drifting through time. They watched as the nurse, tears in her eyes, handed baby James over to a pair of relatives- family members who had come to take him in after the devastating fire. The scene moved swiftly, years passing in an instant, like a fast-forwarded movie. James saw himself growing up, oblivious to the tragic loss of his sister and parents, unaware of the pain and sacrifice that had marked his earliest days. But then, the scene shifted abruptly, and time seemed to rush forward even faster.

Suddenly, James and Arwin found themselves standing in the middle of a hospital room. This time, the atmosphere was eerily quiet. James's heart sank as he recognized the older man lying on the bed- himself, aged and frail, his face etched with the lines of a long, hard life.

James stared in shock at the sight of his future self, his breath catching in his throat. He was much older now, weak and barely able to move. Machines beeped softly around him, monitoring his vital signs. Nurses shuffled quietly in the background, attending to other patients. And then, the sound that pierced the silence-a long, flat tone.

The beeping of the heart monitor stopped, replaced by the unmistakable sound of a flatline. James's heartbeat had stopped. For a moment, time itself seemed to hold its breath. The older James, lying motionless in the hospital bed, had passed away. Nurses rushed to the room, but there was nothing they could do. The scene felt like it was closing in on James and Arwin, the weight of mortality pressing down on them. James, watching this all unfold, was overwhelmed by a deep sense of helplessness.

He couldn't move, couldn't speak. He just stared at his lifeless body, his future self, as the finality of death set in. Arwin, standing beside him, was equally shaken. The reality of what they were witnessing hung heavily in the air.

"Is this... is this how it ends for me?" James asked, his voice barely a whisper, his eyes fixed on his older self lying still in the bed. His heart pounded in his chest, even as he struggled to process the scene before him. Arwin glanced at him, then back at the hospital bed.

"I don't know," he said quietly. "We don't know if this is the future, or just a possibility." James's voice trembled as he spoke, his mind racing. "Why did the universe show us this? Why did it show me my own death?"

"Is this really how it all ends?"

James whispered again, his voice broken. "After everything?"

The hospital scene slowly began to fade, and once again, the two of them were floating in the endless expanse of space. The stars surrounded them like silent witnesses to their grief and the mysteries of the universe. Though James felt broken, he realized that this vision, no matter how painful, was a part of the cosmic journey they were on. He took a deep breath, steadying himself, still haunted by what he had seen but somehow more determined than before.

As the scene of James's lifeless body in the hospital bed began to fade, Arwin and James floated in the quiet emptiness of space, the stars shimmering around them. Both were silent at first, the weight of what they'd just seen hanging over them. Arwin finally spoke, his voice steady, though the gravity of the moment was clear.

"Dr. James... that was hard to watch," Arwin said, his words careful. "But I don't think the universe is showing us this to torture you. There's something deeper here." James, still wiping his tear-streaked face, looked at him.

"But why? Why show me my family's death, a sister I never knew, and then... my own death?" His voice cracked with the pain he couldn't suppress. "I don't understand any of this.

As the scene of Dr. James's death faded, the cosmic vision began to shift. Arwin and James, still floating in space, were suddenly drawn upward, away from Earth. The blue planet below them slowly started to shrink as they drifted farther and farther from its surface. At first, the Earth appeared calm, the familiar continents and oceans spread out below. But then, as the vision accelerated, time seemed to speed up again. The planet began to change-oceans dried up, land masses shifted, and soon, the once-vibrant Earth grew barren and lifeless.

"Is this the end of Earth?" Arwin asked, his voice quiet and filled with a sense of dread.

James nodded, his face pale as he watched the destruction. "It looks like it."

Arwin and James watched in awe as centuries passed in moments. They saw humanity's civilizations rise and fall, cities crumble to dust, and the Earth itself begin to die. The sun, once bright and life-giving, swelled into a massive red giant, its fiery tendrils stretching out into space. The

Earth, now charred and desolate, was engulfed in the sun's expanding flames.

The Earth, now charred and desolate, was engulfed in the sun's expanding flames.

The scene continued to move rapidly, and soon, the Earth was gone- swallowed whole by the dying sun. Arwin and James were left floating in space, the remnants of the solar system barely visible around them. The sun, now a white dwarf, flickered weakly before it, too, faded into the cold darkness of space. But the vision didn't stop there. Time raced forward, the universe expanding raced forward, the universe expanding even faster. Stars around them began to flicker out.

"The sun... it's consuming everything," Arwin muttered, his eyes wide. As the Earth disappeared into the sun, they were pulled further into space, watching as the solar system unraveled. The once-mighty sun, now unstable, collapsed into a small, dim white dwarf, flickering weakly in the darkness of space. But the destruction didn't stop. Time sped up once again. The stars surrounding them began to fade, one by one, their brilliant lights extinguished as they burned through their fuel and died.

The vibrant surface of the sun, with its roiling flames and magnetic storms, began to fade. Arwin and James floated in the cosmic expanse, witnessing the solar collapse unfold before them. They could see the sun swelling into a red giant, its outer layers ballooning outward, engulfing the inner planets, including Earth. The bright light that had once nourished life now turned ominous, casting a blood-red hue across the void. As they got closer, they felt the gravitational forces at play, pulling them toward the sun's fiery surface. The heat intensified, and the air shimmered with the immense energy being released. They witnessed the sun shedding its outer layers, sending brilliant clouds of gas and plasma spiraling into space, creating a stunning yet devastating nebula. In a matter of moments, the sun reached the peak of its expansion, its core compressing under the immense weight of its own gravity.

The light that once illuminated the solar system flickered like a dying candle, signaling that the end was near. Suddenly, with a cataclysmic explosion, the sun went supernova. The shockwave radiated outward at incredible speed, blasting debris into the cosmos. The once-beautiful star was now a chaotic maelstrom of energy and particles, swirling in a cosmic dance. Arwin gasped, watching the remnants of the sun scatter into the darkness.

"This is incredible! But... is it over for the solar system?"

James nodded solemnly. "Yes, this is just the beginning of the end. The supernova will obliterate everything in its vicinity. Earth, Mars, and the other planets won't survive this."

As the shockwave traveled through the solar system, planets were ripped apart, their fragments spiraling into space. The beauty of the solar nebula- composed of colorful gases and dust- was breathtaking but harbored the grim reality of destruction. With each passing moment, the scene accelerated, shifting away from the devastation of the solar system to a broader view of the universe. Arwin and James witnessed countless stars going supernova across the cosmos, one after another. The once-bright galaxies began to flicker, their stars collapsing under the weight of their own gravity, each event echoing the death of their sun.

Time blurred as they saw the universe age rapidly, its once-bustling galaxies now drifting apart in the expanding void. The brilliant lights of distant stars grew dim, and the cosmic dance of creation became a funeral march for the universe.

"Is this how it all ends?" Arwin asked, his voice heavy with despair as they watched the once vibrant universe slip into darkness.

James felt a chill run through him. "Yes, we're witnessing the end of the universe. Without stars, there can be no light, no life. Everything will eventually fade into nothingness." As they floated through the emptiness, the last remnants of energy began to evaporate. The once-mighty galaxies dwindled into faint whispers of their former selves, stars extinguishing one by one until only a cold, dark void remained.

The universe was succumbing to entropy, its final stages marked by the loss of heat and energy. With the stars dying, the vast expanses of space became increasingly silent, with only the remnants of cosmic history lingering in the darkness. Finally, the last flickers of light disappeared, and Arwin and James found themselves surrounded by an infinite emptiness. There was no sound, no light, and no movement-only the profound stillness of a universe that had reached its end. In that endless void, they realized that this was the conclusion of all existence, where even time itself ceased to hold meaning. The universe had come full circle, and all that remained was the chilling silence of nothingness.

They were now left only with memories -fragments of a universe that had once thrived with stars, planets, and life. It felt as if the cosmos was preparing to recreate itself anew, echoing the cycle of existence they had just witnessed. Suddenly, they found themselves back in the same black room from which their journey had begun, a place that felt both familiar and unsettling.

"What is happening?" Arwin's voice trembled with confusion as he glanced around, disoriented by the sudden shift in their surroundings.

"Dr. James, what does all this mean?" His heart raced, grappling with the implications of their experiences.

Dr. James, visibly lost in thought, raised a hand and shouted, "Be quiet! I am thinking!" His brow furrowed, and his eyes narrowed as he sifted through the monumental revelations that had just unfolded before them. The weight of their experiences pressed down on him, but he knew they were on the brink of understanding something profound. After what felt like an eternity in the oppressive silence, Dr. James turned to Arwin, his expression shifting from confusion to clarity.

"I'm beginning to understand what all this signifies," he said slowly, his voice steady yet filled with urgency.

"The universe has crafted this entire narrative so that we can grasp the essence of reality." Arwin's eyes widened, the weight of those words sinking in deeper. "What do you mean?" he asked, his mind racing with possibilities.

Dr. James took a deep breath, drawing strength from the stillness around them. "Nothing is real, Arwin. Nothing! Everything around you is an illusion," he exclaimed, his voice echoing in the vast emptiness.

The gravity of his declaration hung heavily in the air, wrapping around Arwin like a dense fog. He felt a surge of disbelief.

"But we experienced it all! The birth and death of stars, the formation of galaxies—our lives! How can that be an illusion?" Arwin's voice wavered, struggling to comprehend the implications of Dr. James's words.

"Do we have any proof that we've seen all of this?" James asked, his voice tinged with confusion.

"No," Arwin replied, shaking his helmet.

"This is what the universe is trying to show us. We're left with memories, but eventually, those memories fade away. It's like when I was a newborn; I can hardly remember anything from that time, and as I grew, those memories just slipped away." James nodded slowly, reflecting on what Arwin had said. "It's like I was experiencing my own history, but now I realize it's fleeting.

The universe created these moments to show me how I forget things over time. But it's all just an illusion, isn't it?"

"Yes," Arwin confirmed. "That's exactly it. What we see and remember can dissolve into nothingness. The universe constructed this narrative to demonstrate the transient nature of our experiences." We may think we're holding onto something real, but in truth, it's all part of a larger lesson. The universe is guiding us to understand that what we cling to is not the essence of life itself."

A heavy silence fell between them as they absorbed the weight of their conversation. They were confronting the profound truths of existence, grappling with the knowledge that reality might be nothing more than an elaborate illusion. Together, they prepared to face the uncertainty that lay ahead, ready to embrace whatever came next in their journey through the cosmos.

"Reality is just like a game created by the universe," James continued, his voice steady but laced with a sense of urgency.

"Now, the universe will repeat itself. The Big Bang will happen again, and everything we know will come to an end. All our hate and love will fade away, just like memories slipping through our fingers and we're just players in this cosmic game."

Suddenly, the universe began to stir anew, signaling the start of another cycle. This time, however, James and Arwin were acutely aware of the reality they had just witnessed. A radiant white light surged forward, spreading throughout the entire room, illuminating every shadow and corner with its intense glow. It was so blindingly bright that they instinctively shut their eyes, shielding themselves from its brilliance.

"What is this now?" Arwin asked, his voice tinged with a mix of awe and confusion as he tried to comprehend the overwhelming spectacle.

Now, the light had dimmed enough for them to fully open their eyes. The once blinding brightness had softened, allowing them to take in their surroundings more clearly.

As they opened their eyes, a white light spread around them, revealing what they had assumed was a black room. However, as the light grew brighter, the truth became clear. Before them stood a massive gate, towering and imposing, marking the path ahead. What they had first thought was a dark, enclosed space was something far more mysterious.

"What is happening now?" Arwin asked, his voice steady but tense.

"I don't know," James replied, "but whatever it is, it's trying to tell us something."

The white light surrounded them completely, soft and all-encompassing, yet in front of them stood the door- silent and unmoving, the only clear shape in this strange void.

"Are we in a dream... or did we die?" Arwin's voice was barely above a whisper, his eyes fixed on the strange scene around them.

The endless expanse of white light, the stillness in the air, and the imposing door ahead gave everything an otherworldly quality. James didn't respond right away, his gaze locked on the massive door.

Instead, he took a deep breath and said, "Arwin, follow me." Without waiting for an answer, James started walking, his footsteps seeming to echo in the emptiness. Arwin hesitated only for a moment before falling into step beside him. The vast, silent space around them felt unnerving, but the door ahead drew them forward like a magnetic pull. Each step they took seemed to bring the door closer, its dark frame cutting through the light like a shadow. Neither of them spoke as they approached, the air thick with the weight of something unknown waiting on the other side.

As they reached the door, it creaked open as if it had a will of its own, swinging wide to reveal a scene that defied comprehension. Arwin and Dr. James stepped through,

their hearts racing with anticipation.
What lay beyond the threshold was astonishing-a vast expanse that felt both infinite and intimate, a floating library suspended in a realm of ethereal light. Books of all shapes and sizes floated gracefully in the air, their spines adorned with titles that shimmered in the soft glow. The sight was mesmerizing, like a constellation of stories and knowledge, each volume drifting gently as if buoyed by an unseen force.
Arwin, barely able to contain his wonder, gazed around in awe.

"What is this place?" he breathed, eyes wide.

Dr. James observed the surroundings, a mixture of curiosity and caution flickering in his expression. "It seems to be a library-one unlike any I've ever encountered. The books... they're suspended in mid-air."
The air was thick with the scent of old paper and ink, a comforting aroma that brought a rush of nostalgia to the doctor, even as it struck Arwin as oddly familiar yet foreign. This was no ordinary library; the books seemed alive, swirling in a delicate ballet, their pages fluttering softly as if whispering secrets to one another.
Tentatively, Dr. James stepped forward, the floor beneath them indistinguishable from the vast nothingness surrounding them.

"Keep close, Arwin," he cautioned, glancing back at the young boy. "We don't know what we're dealing with here."

As soon as they stepped through the threshold, the gate behind them slammed shut with a thunderous boom, sealing them inside the surreal, floating library. Arwin spun around, eyes wide in alarm as he stared at the now-closed entrance.

"The gate... it just closed," he muttered, his voice barely above a whisper.

Dr. James, though taken aback, kept his focus forward.

"Don't worry about it. Stay close. We need to figure out what this place is." His voice remained steady, but there was an undercurrent of caution in his words.

They ventured further into the heart of the strange library, where thousands of books drifted around them in mid-air, weightless and silent. It was like nothing Arwin had ever seen before-an endless space with no walls or ceiling, just an infinite sea of knowledge suspended in a a strange, otherworldly light. The soft rustle of fluttering pages filled the air, creating an eerie, whisper-like atmosphere.

Arwin's gaze darted from one book to the next, his steps slowing as he absorbed the surreal environment. Then, something caught his eye. He stopped suddenly, his heart racing.

"Look," he said, pointing toward one of the books floating nearby.

"That one... it's following us." Dr. James turned, following Arwin's gaze. A single book seemed to hover a little closer than the others, moving subtly in their direction each time they took a step.

"Keep calm," Dr. James murmured, though he too was fixated on the strange behavior of the book. "It might just be part of the illusion."

They resumed walking, but the book continued to follow them, trailing behind as if observing their every move.It was unsettling, a silent presence that neither of them could shake.

As they moved deeper into the vast space, the book began to drift closer, breaking away from the others. At first, it moved slowly, almost tentatively, but then its pace quickened. Without warning, it darted toward them with sudden urgency.

Arwin's pulse quickened, and he stepped back instinctively. "What's it doing?" he asked, his voice shaky.

Dr. James remained rooted in place, watching intently as the book came to a stop just inches from them, floating in mid-air. Its cover hung open, and before either of them could react, the pages began turning-slowly at first, then faster and faster, the sound of rustling paper growing louder with each passing second. The once-quiet flutter now resembled a frantic storm, as if the book was desperate to reveal something hidden within its pages.

Arwin's voice trembled as he spoke. "It's... it's like it's trying to tell us something."

Dr. James stared at the book, his face tense with concentration. "Maybe it is."

XIII

As Arwin and Dr. James stood transfixed by the book, the once still pages began to shimmer, the ink fading in and out like something alive. Then, without warning, the text disappeared altogether, and the book's surface started to glow. Slowly, images began to emerge from the open pages, not printed words, but full scenes as though a story was unfolding before them-alive and in motion.

Arwin gasped as the book projected what looked like a moving picture, floating just above its pages. It was like watching a hologram, but it felt real.

As the holographic scene unfolded before them, the first image that appeared wasn't of a fantastical place or ancient symbols-it was a hospital room. The rush of nurses and doctors filled the space, their hurried movements betraying the seriousness of the situation. In the center of it all was a patient lying motionless on a bed, eyes closed, surrounded by a tangle of machines beeping in rhythm with the person's fragile breathing. Arwin furrowed his brow, confused by what he was seeing.

"Why is the book showing us someone's story?" he asked, his voice low.

Dr. James watched the scene with growing intensity.

"No," he said after a moment, "this isn't just a random story. It must have a connection to us."

Before Arwin could ask more, a voice emerged from the hologram, soft yet filled with emotion.

"Dr. Arwin, please get well soon. We need you back... we need you."

Arwin's face tightened in disbelief. His mind raced. Dr. Arwin?

The figure in the bed-pale, motionless-was him. He could hear the sobs of those surrounding the bed, people he didn't recognize, their faces twisted in grief.

"This is nonsense!" Arwin shouted, stepping back from the glowing book. "This book is fake-just trying to mess with us!" but Dr. James didn't respond to his outburst. His eyes remained locked on the image, focused. Silent.

The voice from the hologram spoke again, weaker this time.

"We need you back soon." A woman's tear-streaked face blurred into view, her voice breaking as she spoke. The entire room seemed consumed by sadness, the people gathered around the bed clinging to hope that was rapidly slipping away.

Suddenly, the doors to the room swung open, and a doctor entered. His expression was grave, his footsteps heavy. One of the women turned to him with desperation in her eyes.

"Dr. James, will you be able to save Dr. Arwin?" she asked, her voice barely holding back the panic. "We've never seen a case progress this rapidly." Dr. James exhaled, looking down at the chart he held in his hands.

"Quantum Cellular Decay Syndrome is... well, it's almost impossible to treat with the technology we have." His words were measured, careful, but the weight behind them was unmistakable.

"The body's cells are breaking down at the quantum level. It's like the very fabric of his existence is unraveling." The women's eyes widened. "But there's hope, right?"

Dr. James shook his head, his voice heavy with resignation. "The degeneration is irreversible with our current medical knowledge. I don't know if we can save him."

As the hologram continued to display the scene in the hospital room, his frustration boiled over.

"This is nonsense!" Arwin shouted, stepping back from the floating book.

His face flushed with anger. "Kelvin is my friend! He's the one who's sick, not me! What kind of trick is this?"

Dr. James stood silent, still focused on the scene unfolding before them, but Arwin's mind was racing. He pointed at the book, his voice rising. "This is all backwards! It's showing the wrong story. I'm not the one in that bed- Kelvin is. This book is a lie!"

His heart pounded as he stared at the image of himself lying pale and lifeless on the hospital bed. . Everything about it felt wrong, like a cruel distortion of reality.

People crying, voices whispering his name, praying for his recovery. It wasn't supposed to be him. Kelvin had been diagnosed with Quantum Cellular Decay Syndrome, not him. How could the book mix that up?

Arwin's fists clenched in frustration, but Dr. James remained composed, his eyes still locked on the projection. "Arwin..." he said softly, his tone unreadable.

"I don't think this is a mistake." Arwin turned on him, incredulous. "What do you mean, not a mistake'?

The book is wrong. This isn't my story. It's Kelvin's!"

The woman collapsed onto the bed, clutching Dr. Arwin's frail body, her sobs loud and raw.

"This isn't possible," she cried, her voice breaking with every word.

Arwin stirred, his eyelids heavy, his voice barely a whisper.

"Why does it feel like I've seen her before?" he murmured, more to himself than anyone else. Dr. James, standing nearby, glanced sharply at him.

"Seen her where?" he asked, his tone calm but probing. Arwin's brow furrowed, his eyes searching for something just out of reach. "I don't know... I can't remember."

As the the continued, the man appeared older, in his twenties, tall and strong, with features that seemed so familiar yet different, more mature.

Then it hit him.

“Kelvin!” Arwin shouted, his voice trembling with shock. “This looks like Kelvin!”

His mind reeled. The Kelvin he knew was younger, his best friend, but this version of him was somehow older, transformed.

Kelvin sat hunched over in the sterile hospital room, his small frame trembling. Tears streamed down his cheeks, falling relentlessly onto his clenched fists. Dr. James's words echoed in his mind, each syllable hitting him like a blow.

“We can't save Dr. Arwin.”

The weight of those words crushed him. Kelvin gasped for breath between sobs, his chest heaving as he tried to make sense of it. "No, no..." he whimpered, his voice breaking.

The scene shifted to later that night, when the world outside had gone quiet and the weight of the day's events became unbearable. Kelvin sat alone in the darkness of his room, his chest heaving with silent sobs. The grief he'd held back all day finally broke through, and tears streamed down his face as he thought of Dr. Arwin-his friend, his mentor-lying helpless, fighting against something they couldn't yet understand.

As the night deepened, after Kelvin had cried himself into a hollow silence over Dr. Arwin's fate, he finally succumbed to an exhausted sleep. But even in his slumber, his mind could not find peace.

In his dream, the scene unfolded vividly. A young boy, running desperately through shadowy streets, his breath coming in sharp, frantic bursts. He reached a house at the end of the road, fear and urgency driving him forward.

He pounded on the door with his fists, his voice trembling as he cried out, "Dr. James! Dr. James!"

Suddenly, Arwin's voice pierced through the dream, frantic and full of confusion. "That's me!" he shouted, his heart racing with the sudden recognition. "This is the morning I was coming to your house... I wanted to tell you about my dream! The one where I found the reason-how to save Kelvin!"

The air around them seemed to thicken, the dream blurring the line between reality and memory. Arwin's voice grew more urgent as he realized what was unfolding before him.

"It means... my reality was the dream for Kelvin?" His voice shook with disbelief, trying to grasp the impossible connection.

In the midst of a dream, Arwin turned to Dr. James, his voice urgent. "I have to see your storeroom," he insisted, eyes filled with determination. "Antimatter is the solution!"

Kelvin jolted awake, his heart pounding in his chest, beads of sweat clinging to his skin. His breath came in ragged gasps, and his eyes darted around the dimly lit room, struggling to shake off the lingering terror from his dream. Suddenly the words echoed in Kelvin's mind, his heart pounding in his chest. What could possibly be in that storeroom? His face reflected a tumult of fear and hope. Dr. Arwin had often said that dreams were intertwined with reality.

"I need to go to that room," he murmured to himself, a sense of purpose igniting within him.

Without wasting another moment, he grabbed his phone and called a friend for a ride. Minutes later, a car pulled up, and Kelvin rushed outside.

As he approached the vehicle, disbelief washed over.

Arwin shouted, "Dr. James! This is my physics teacher—Caldwell!" behind the wheel, the same one who had always made the subject feel like a tedious chore. A strange twist of fate, he thought shaking his head at the irony.

They arrived at the house that had dominated his dream, and Kelvin approached the owner with a mix of anxiety and determination.

"Could we please look at your storeroom?" he asked, his voice steady despite the pounding of his heart.

The owner shook his head, his expression firm. "No, that's not possible."

Disappointment clawed at Kelvin, but he quickly scanned the surroundings and spotted a broken window at the side of the house. Inspiration struck.

"I'll go in," he said resolutely. He turned to his friend, urgency clear in his voice. "You stay here. It's not safe."

The air around them seemed to thicken, the dream blurring the line between reality and memory. Arwin's voice grew more urgent as he realized what was unfolding before him.

"It means... my reality was the dream for Kelvin?" Arwin's voice shook with disbelief, trying to grasp the impossible connection.

"Yes, Arwin. Yes," came the quiet, assured voice of Dr. James, who seemed to stand just on the edge of the dream, watching everything unfold with newfound clarity. "I understand now. Everything makes sense."

Then the scene continued, Kelvin stepped through the threshold into the dimly lit room, a jolt of realization struck him, sending chills down his spine. At that moment, Arwin's voice burst forth, laden with urgency and an edge of panic.

"This is my dream! I am watching my dream again!" he shouted, his gaze fixed on Dr. James, whose expression mirrored disbelief.

James stood frozen, shock washing over him in waves. His mind raced to comprehend the surreal nature of the moment, grappling with the bizarre connection that seemed to tie them all together. The gravity of Arwin's declaration settled heavily in the air, suffocating and electrifying all at once. Suddenly, the owner of the house stormed in, his face a mixture of anger and bewilderment as he caught sight of Kelvin rummaging through the room.

"What are you doing in here?" he barked, stepping forward with a menacing air, demanding an explanation. Without hesitation, Kelvin turned to face the man, fueled by the urgency of the situation.

"Antimatter is the solution!" he declared, his voice steady yet filled with fervor. The words felt like a spark igniting a fire, an instinctive response to the chaos that swirled around them.

Outside, Kelvin's friend's voice rang out, filled with desperation. "Come on, Kelvin! We have to hurry!" The urgency in the tone made Kelvin's heart race faster, a reminder that time was slipping away, and every second counted in their quest for answers.

"I'm coming!" Kelvin shouted back, determination surging within him. The world around him blurred for a moment as he focused on the task ahead, the sensation of being on the precipice of something monumental engulfing him.

With Arwin's words echoing in his mind, a sense of destiny washed over him. He knew they were standing on the brink of a crucial revelation, one that could change everything. The tension in the library crackled like electricity, and he felt the weight of responsibility pressing down on him. As he readied himself to push forward, he caught a glimpse of James, whose eyes were wide with a mix of shock and hope. In that instant, Arwin understood that they were all bound by a shared purpose, racing against time to unlock the mysteries that lay hidden within the house.

As the final page of the book turned and closed with a resounding thud, an eerie silence enveloped the library. The air felt charged, heavy with the weight of unspoken truths. James and Arwin exchanged pale, bewildered glances, their hearts racing as they processed the revelations that had just shattered their understanding of reality.

"Do you understand?" Arwin asked, his voice barely rising above a whisper, his eyes wide with a mix of fear and curiosity. He turned to James, searching for a glimmer of comprehension in his face.

"Yes, Arwin," James replied, his voice trembling. "Everything." The shock hung in the air like a thick fog, blurring the lines between what they had always known and the startling truths now laid bare before them.

"This universe is far more surprising than we can fathom," James said, shaking his head in disbelief. His thoughts tumbled over one another, colliding in a chaotic storm. Doubt gnawed at him, eroding the foundation of his beliefs. The comforting certainties of his life felt fragile and precarious, as if they could shatter at any moment.

"The story we saw was not just a story," he murmured, his voice gaining strength with each word. "It was real." The tremor in his tone belied the monumental implications of their discovery, sending chills down his spine. Arwin nodded slowly, his mind racing to catch up with the gravity of what they had uncovered.

"The narrative we witnessed-it came from a different universe," he said, each word deliberate, as if trying to solidify this newfound truth.

"Where you are a brilliant scientist, and I'm just a doctor. You were diagnosed with Quantum Cellular Decay Syndrome, and Kelvin came to save you."

As the pieces fell into place, the reality of parallel universes settled heavily on their shoulders, transforming the ordinary into the extraordinary. The implications twisted in their minds, turning familiarity into something unrecognizable.

"So it means that parallel universes truly exist," Arwin breathed, his voice barely above a whisper, the enormity of the concept sending shivers down his spine. James stared at him, his own eyes wide with the dawning realization.

"Today, I learned that nothing is real," he declared, his voice shaking with a mixture of dread and wonder. "You, me -nothing." The words hung in the air, reverberating with existential weight, shaking the very core of their identities.

"We are merely creations of the universe, drifting toward nothingness. This is what the universe was trying to convey."

Suddenly, Arwin's expression shifted, his eyes wide with astonishment. "Dr. James," he said, his voice almost a whisper," the staff member at the hospital where Kelvin was admitted- which hugged me, I remember now! She was the one who gave me a ride to your home when I came to find a solution for Kelvin!" James's heart raced as he processed Arwin's revelation.

It means that everything we've experienced, every encounter we've had, is somehow linked to another reality!" Arwin's voice trembled with excitement and shock. "In that world, she is my partner, and I can't believe we're connected like this.

"All of this-what you're doing, what you're chasing-it's part of illusion. said james surprisingly.

He leaned forward, watching Arwin closely. But I still have some questions."

He paused, as if choosing his words carefully. "What's the connection of antimatter with all this?"

Arwin looked up, surprised by the question.

As if responding to his inquiry, the book that had just closed floated away, vanishing into the dim corners of the library. In its place, another book appeared from the shadows, drifting toward them and opening with a soft whisper. To their surprise, its pages were blank.

"What does it mean?"

Arwin asked, bewildered. After a tense moment, the blank pages shimmered, and a voice emerged from within. "Your universe is made up of matter, while theirs is constructed from antimatter. They need matter to save Arwin, and you need antimatter to save Kelvin."

James took a deep breath, a mix of hope and dread filling him. "One more question," he ventured cautiously. "Are my parents living happily in this universe? They loved each other so much." The book hesitated before responding, its tone somber. "In this universe, they don't even know each other."

Suddenly, a low rumble echoed through the air, growing steadily louder as the walls began to tremble. James and Arwin exchanged frantic glances, the weight of their discoveries still heavy in their minds. Before they could comprehend what was happening, the library around them began to shrink, the once-spacious room collapsing inward like a dying star. Shelves filled with books warped and distorted, their contents vanishing into the void as if consumed by an unseen force. The ground beneath their feet felt unstable, rippling like water, and the very air crackled with energy."What's happening?" Arwin shouted, his voice barely rising above the chaos.

James reached for Arwin's arm, his eyes wide with fear. "I think we're being pulled back! Hold on!"

The white light flared again, growing so intense that Arwin and James instinctively covered their eyes. It was blinding, sharper than before, as if the light itself was alive, pulsing with energy. Arwin could feel his heart racing, his mind spinning with uncertainty.

"Where are we going now?" Arwin managed to ask, his voice barely audible over the roar of the light.

James didn't answer. He didn't need to. They were both caught in the same surreal whirlwind, with no control over what would happen next. The sensation of being pulled somewhere else filled Arwin with a strange mix of fear and curiosity. His feet no longer felt grounded, as if the world had dissolved beneath them.

And then, just as suddenly as it had appeared, the light vanished.

Arwin blinked a few times, his vision adjusting to the sudden shift in brightness. The cool, sterile scent hit his nose first. He glanced around and realized they were standing in a small, dimly lit hospital washroom. White tiles lined the floor and walls, a sink and mirror in front of them. Water dripped faintly from the faucet, echoing in the quiet room.

"Are we back?" Arwin asked, still disoriented. James ran a hand through his hair, his face a mixture of confusion and cautious relief.

"Maybe..." he replied, though his voice, muffled inside the helmet of his space suit, didn't carry much certainty.

They cautiously pushed open the door and stepped into the hospital hallway.

People freeze mid-step, mouths slightly open as they take in the sight of two figures covered head to toe in gleaming space gear, helmets reflecting the sterile fluorescent lights. The fluorescent lights overhead buzzed softly, casting a cold glow on the linoleum floor. The air smelled of disinfectant and something faintly metallic.

Nurses and doctors moved hurriedly in the distance, but everything felt slightly off, like a strange calm before a storm. Then they heard it-someone shouting.

"Kelvin is safe! The damaged cells... they're repairing themselves!" Dr. Lenox's voice rang out, sharp and astonished. He stood at the far end of the corridor, his white coat flaring as he gestured wildly to a group of doctors around him. His face was a mix of disbelief and triumph.

As his eyes met James', he saw it reflected back at him-the same realization, the same quiet understanding. James wasn't confused or panicked. In fact, he seemed calm, almost serene. James and Arwin stood there, in the middle of the impossibility, and neither spoke a word.

And then, without meaning to, they smiled at each other. It wasn't a smile of joy or relief, but a soft, knowing smile. Like they both understood that none of this-none of the hospital, the shouting doctor, the miracle recovery-was just the illiusion.

www.ingramcontent.com/pod-product-compliance
Lightning Source LLC
LaVergne TN
LVHW091049150826
845673LV00002B/513

9798895563137